THE DARK OF THE SEA

Imam BAKSH

Blouse & Skirt Books

KINGSTON AND NEW JERSEY

© Imam Baksh 2019

First published by Blouse & Skirt Books, 2019

Blouse & Skirt Books is an imprint of Blue Banyan Books Ltd.

A CIP catalogue record of this book is available from the National Library of Jamaica

ISBN 978-976-8267-23-8

Cover and book design by Ion Communications
Cover art by Richard Nattoo

Blue Banyan Books
PO Box 5464
Liguanea PO
Kingston 6, Jamaica

www.bluebanyanbooks.com

Thanks are due to CODE, The Burt Award for Caribbean Young Adult Literature and the Bocas Literary Festival

ACKNOWLEDGEMENTS

Thanks to Aadil for urging me to write this book and to my editor, Tanya Batson-Savage, for shaping it.

For my constant companions,

Aadil

Mariam

Saarah

Raheel

Akhtar

Maraiyah

THE DARK OF THE SEA

Imam Baksh

Blouse & Skirt Books
KINGSTON

PROLOGUE

The top of the massive wave gleamed foamy silver on the far horizon as the wall of dark water built and coiled towards the shore.

It still had some way to come – there was a mile of muddy, exposed shore where the ocean had been sucked out to feed the approaching tsunami. Danesh knew all about how that worked. Over the last month, he had heard many legends of inundations and cataclysms. The boy stood on the cracked and flaking concrete seawall, wearing just his torn jeans and his ever-present rubber sandals. In the old tales, the hero would be standing as tall as the wave, wearing godly armor and loaded with magic charms. His muscles would ripple and his many weapons sing for battle ... as his hair whipped in the wind and he roared bravely.

But Danesh was short, with all the muscles of a coconut sapling. He had no weapon. Nothing but the rocky spine of the treacherous *Book of Eibon*, digging into his hipbone as he wondered if he dared open it and risk the misty rain on its ancient ink or the howling wind against its fragile parchments.

But it was Danesh's duty to end the oncoming disaster. All he had to do was flawlessly read an entire page in an ancient and unknown language. Never mind that he had never managed to read even a sentence of English correctly at school. Never mind the rain, the wind and the meagre illumination of the moonlight.

The sun should have been up. Every clock on the coast had stopped working at midnight, but Danesh knew there should be sunlight by now. Yet the stars still shone, eerie behind the shroud of white-streaked clouds that stretched overhead like spiderwebs.

So it was just them: Danesh, the wave, and the darkness.

Oh, and the hundred or so scaly, frog-faced, mutant-men slouching through the muck towards the shore so that they could slaughter his friends and neighbours.

> *On a night without dawn the*
> *dark of the sea comes to*
> *end mankind's reign and still*
> *the pulse of Earthly life*

That was Eibon's vision, set down by his crawling pen a hundred thousand years before, now made real before the eyes of a lone fifteen-year-old boy.

The first time Danesh ever saw the dark of the sea was the night of the fireworks.

He and Amit had wanted a good view of the show and the water tank tower in Amit's yard was an easy climb. Danesh complained about it anyway.

"You can't put a ladder pon this thing?" he asked as he pulled himself up the second concrete cross-post, about ten feet above the ground where Surwa the dog was resentfully watching them.

Amit looked down from near the top of the two-story tower. "Is not two good hand and two good foot you got?"

"That's not the point. You backside only giving me—" Danesh squealed and cursed, having reached his hand up and grasped the cold, bumpy flesh of a toad.

"What happen with you now?" Amit asked, amused. He was already on the platform with the two black water tanks.

"You got *crappo* up here." Danesh wiped his hand on the rough edge of the concrete, scraping it clean of – he wasn't sure what, exactly – and tried to make his voice deep to hide his shame at how he had reacted earlier. "How *crappo* even reach up here?"

"I got a special ladder for *crappo*." Amit sat on the edge, swinging his legs like a little child. "Still no ladder for you though."

Danesh sucked his teeth and moved left to avoid the toad he had touched, watching where he put his hand each time. He levered himself easily around the corner to the adjoining face of the tower and climbed up without speaking. At the top, he stood on the rectangle of unpainted wooden planks. The plastic tanks which rested there were two feet taller than him, holding water that had been pumped up so the house could have running water on the second floor. Almost every house in Essequibo had a tower like this in the backyard because the water mains never had much pressure.

"Here," said Danesh, sitting next to his friend and swiping his palm against Amit's face, "Take back you *crappo* juice."

"Hey, behave you'self before I throw you off this place." Amit grinned and pointed a finger at him. "Don't think that 'cause I save you life one time I won't kill you if you make me vex."

This again.

Back when they were seven, the two boys had started 'borrowing' some of the smaller fishing boats at the koker channel when their owners were distracted. Until the day a stiff wave had upended Danesh into the water.

The way Amit always told the story, he had heroically gone hunting for Danesh's unconscious body and brought him back from near drowning. Danesh never contradicted him because the way he remembered things, well he must have indeed blacked out and been dreaming.

Hitting the water that day had jarred his eyes into seeing everything. The mud brown water of the Essequibo Coast became glass clear. He could see fish swimming in silver flashes all around him. Feel the heat of life from crabs digging under the grey silt. And he could breathe! Danesh had felt so comfortable in the water that he had chosen to float in its relaxing cushion, even giggling as he watched Amit desperately searching for him, one hand on the edge of the boat while he tried to peer through the opaque water with a desperate grimace and flung his other arm around to grab his lost friend.

It was only when Danesh realised that Amit was about to let go of the boat and come down for him that he had relented from his joke and let himself be 'rescued'.

And now his debt was a cornerstone of Amit's claim to him as a friend. One Danesh couldn't contradict, no matter how annoying the frequent reminders were.

Danesh gazed out towards Georgetown. The city itself

was beyond the horizon, on the other side of the Essequibo River's mouth, but the glow from its lights hovered above the water to the south-east.

The ocean was calm as midnight approached. There was no moon but light rippled merrily across its surface, reflected from a hundred bright stars. On the arc of the clear horizon the lights of four shrimp boats stood out, looking like fallen stars floating on the water. One of those boats was probably his father's but Danesh didn't attach any significance to that. He tended not to give thought to the world beyond his immediate surroundings.

To their left was the shadow shape of the big koker, the sluice-way that drained the rice lands into the sea when the tide was out. A few coconut trees beyond that was the hang-out shack the local teens had been gradually erecting over the past two years. Amit and Danesh would have been down there now, except for Amit's obsession with seeing the Independence Day fireworks.

"You sure about this?" Danesh asked. "It so far–"

"I telling you. I see it last year. Clear."

"So why you got fo' see it again?"

"Fiftieth Independence, man. They say in the news that it gon' be a big celebration. Can't miss that."

Music drifted down from Norah's rum shop. A chutney song of course. The singer's girlfriend didn't love him anymore so he was going to drink rum until he died.

"You get them Ravi B tickets yet?" Danesh asked.

"Nah, work got me bad these days. The concert not for a while though, so I gon' get them when I got a day off."

Out on the water, a dark blur bothered Danesh. He got dizzy looking at the sea sometimes, years now since his near 'drowning'. His vision would shimmer and then it was like he could see through the water. See *beyond* it. The idea of going beyond anything made him nervous.

But this dark in the sea tonight bothered him for the opposite reason. It seemed impenetrable and dangerous.

The song at the rum shop changed. The new singer was telling his girlfriend's father that it was okay that the man wasn't allowing them to get married. Because it meant more time for the singer to drink rum.

The thought of forbidden love prompted Danesh to ask, "What happening with Susie?"

"Nothing. She mother and father still acting crazy, telling she they gon' call the police fo' lock me up and all that."

"So what you gon' do?"

"Same as ever. Every morning I pass them when I going to work, I gon' say, 'Good morning,' and I gone me way in peace. I ain't got time for stress."

Over in the shack, a cell phone lit up briefly. Their friends were probably down there right now, smoking cigarettes and other things.

"The job thing working out though?"

Amit didn't reply. He had dropped out of school two months before, as soon as he was legally allowed to. Being fifteen as well, Danesh was already old enough to follow him. His friend seemed to have spending money these days and, more importantly, freedom from the demands of school and parents, but his silence wasn't a good sign.

But that was probably just because he was having trouble in his love life.

A Whistling Thunder went off in the next village. Danesh didn't care for the screech of the little rocket or the abrupt explosion of the illegal firecracker it had boosted into the air, but the rumbling murmur afterward as the air settled with an *mmmbmmbm* sat well in his soul for some reason.

More whistles and bangs called out as midnight arrived.

Surwa's black and white shape slinked off to hide from the noise. Across the sea, a pink burst of light signalled the start of the fireworks being launched from the unseen city below. The spark was smaller than a fingernail held at arm's length. A green flash burst next to it. Then two yellow ones, each popping silently.

"Too bad we can't be there close up," said Amit. "Them thing does be impressive how they loud. I wish they coulda give we a li'l fireworks down here. But is like them Georgetown people don't believe Essequibo is really part of Guyana."

Surwa the dog emerged below now that the squibs and fireworks had gone quiet in the neighborhood. He checked that the boys were still safe up above and then got into barking at a hefty toad as it hopped along in the drain near the fence.

"Hmm," said Amit. "You might got a point 'bout them *crappo*. Been seeing a lot of them recently."

"Probably just 'cause of the rainy season is all," Danesh answered, only half paying attention. He was staring at the dark spot in the water. He could see someone swimming there whenever a firework went off. But that didn't make sense. It was much too far away. And who went swimming at night anyway?

After about fifteen minutes, the fireworks were over, leaving a haze of smoke thousands of feet high that glowed in the city lights. Danesh tried not to show how unimpressed he had been with the whole thing for Amit's sake.

But it was his friend who said, "End up being kind of small, eh? All that talk about celebrating fifty years as a country and nothing didn't really happen."

As they descended, Norah's rum shop played them another tune. This singer was telling his wife that she shouldn't complain about him staying out late because she'd always known he was a drinker. The song was still stuck in his head when he fell asleep ten minutes later.

The next morning, the dead whale washed ashore.

He left home already ten minutes late, having put on his school uniform like a prisoner headed to break rocks. The only thing that Danesh had taken any care over was setting each spiked strand of hair in place at the front. He thought about removing the glass bead 'diamond' stud he wore in his ear but decided he would keep on looking stylish until he was actually at the schoolyard. Since his mother was in the front, tending to the hibiscus plants around her new concrete altar, Danesh left through the door in the unpainted back half of the house. He opened the back gate with its wrought iron ॐ symbol declaring the house's residents to be Hindus, then crossed the plank set over the bushy back drain and circled around to the main road.

The whole village seemed strangely silent, with just Shivani Ramgopal checking messages on her phone while she waited to catch a taxi to school. Shivani was actually Danesh's cousin, but ever since their grandfather had bribed a Ministry official last year to get her a place at the 'good' school several villages away, they hardly spoke. Which was too bad, Danesh thought – the girl knew a lot of dirty jokes, and more importantly, she knew how to tell them the juiciest way.

Nobody was at Aunty Pinky's phulourie stall. Not even Aunty Pinky. And a further blanket of isolation came from the rainy season sky which extended a grey haze from one end of the straight road to the other.

Up near Norah's empty rum shop, a small shape resembling an alien antelope crossed the road with nervous steps. When Danesh got close, he found it to be a stray dog, licking up stale vomit from the concrete where some drunk had thoughtfully left it the night before. The dog's body seemed like it was made of just shoulders, spine and hips draped with a burnt carpet. The animal kept its head bowed in shame until he passed.

"Danesh!" shouted a young voice. This was Clarendon, a kindergartener, who had decided several months ago that Danesh was his best friend. The boy was standing on the footpath that lead to the rocky shore. On the opposite side of the main road, Danesh caught sight of Miss Lily and the other teachers inside the low kindergarten building, teaching the students who hadn't given themselves permission to leave. Clarendon said, "Danesh, you not coming fo' see the whale!?"

Danesh's first instinct was to wave the annoying child off, but the word 'whale' penetrated and he started running up the path himself.

"Carry me! Carry me!" Clarendon shouted as Danesh neared. As much as he disliked the boy, it seemed only fair to reward him for letting Danesh know about the new arrival.

Still, the boy was heavy for Danesh and he struggled through the loose sand before he got to the solid ground at the top of the sea dam.

The massive black and grey carcass lay at the high-water mark, where the narrow strip of sand that crowded the boulders of the seawall gave way to grey-brown mud. The whale was on its side, one giant fin in the air. One milky eye, as large as Danesh's head, stared at the cloudy sky.

Even from a distance, Danesh could tell the beast had died in battle. Jagged rips were slashed into its side and their shape and placement spoke to him of malice.

He wondered for a moment why the villagers had formed a wall at a distance from the body rather than moving close and touching it. But when he walked closer, the stench hit him.

"Oh Lord," said Clarendon giggling. "That thing smell worse than Miss Lily armpit."

The whale was freshly killed. In fact, Danesh was sure now that this was the shape he had seen drifting in the ocean the night before. Strange that it should already be so rotten. Over to his right, a few disappointed men were walking away with hatchets, cutlasses and empty buckets.

Small hands pulled at Danesh's belt. Clarendon again, loud and insistent. "Is how big is it, Danesh? Measure it and see!"

Edging as close as he could tolerate, Danesh walked a path parallel to the dead whale. Twenty-seven steps. Now that he was standing near the tail end, Danesh admired the gentle swoop of the tail. He pictured this animal in motion beneath the waves, easing itself along like–

"Clarendon!"

Miss Lily had come to the waterside to reclaim her escapee. Time for Danesh to head to school too. The whale would still be here this afternoon. He took a last look back to see the teacher chasing Clarendon around the other side of the carcass and then he turned south, deciding to walk to school along the sea dam.

To his left, across a wide stretch of water, was the start of Tiger Island. It was an abandoned place, visible as a bushy line of dark trees that ran parallel to the coast for about four miles.

As he watched the brown wave tops of the river break into silver flashes, Danesh again felt like he could sense someone swimming just beyond his vision.

The stench of the whale followed him to school and grew throughout the day. By morning break, the students were sniffing the air and making disgusted faces at each other.

Their disgust wasn't enough to put them off food, however. They crowded against the counter where the school canteen sold snacks and drinks. Danesh held his cash folded lengthwise, hoping the supply of plantain chips hadn't sold out already.

"Nobody don't beg!" Robot walked into the cafeteria. Not even the teachers called the boy Nicholas anymore. He was tall, with a loose afro – in which he kept a long-toothed comb. In one hand was a small paper bag giving off the spicy scent of the plantain chips he had smuggled in from a street vendor. As he walked with an exaggerated chip-step he kept the other hand up, palm open in a blocking position. "I ain't got nothing for no beggar-man, so keep all you mouth shut."

"Robot," said a girl standing in line, "nobody don't want you dirty plantain no how."

Nadira was an old enemy of Robot's. In fact, it was she who had first called him 'Robot' back in Grade 4. A whip-shaped girl, her neck swayed as she spoke. "God know the whole bag must be cover in spit from all what you talking with you slobbery mouth."

"Alright," answered Robot. "That's one beggar-man open they mouth." He pointed at Nadira. "I mark you down."

"Who beg?!"

Robot ignored her and turned to Danesh. "*You* ain't beg. If you ask nice, I gon' give you some."

"Who beg!?" Nadira had left her knot of friends and was halfway to Robot now, hand on hip while he continued to ignore her.

Danesh looked at the greasy bag. "How nice I got fo' ask?"

"Sweet like you mouth make with sugar."

Nadira was shouting in Robot's ear now, but he kept his eyes locked with Danesh.

"Robot," Danesh said, "Please..." He grabbed the bag from Robot's hand and shouted, "Please don't bother me with you and Nadira rickiticks and dramatics." He handed the bag to the girl and said, "Take this gift as you skin so shine and you teeth so straight."

Nadira stuck her tongue out at Robot as she palmed the bag. He reached for it and Danesh took the money in his hand and whipped him across the forehead with the two blue bills.

"Get back," he said.

At first Robot seemed angry, then Danesh whipped him again. "Bad dog. Get back."

By the third time Danesh struck him, Robot had gotten the joke and lowered his head while making growling noises.

As Danesh and the children near him erupted into laughter, Nadira flicked her hair and walked away, saying, "Keep

13

you dog pon he chain, Danesh, otherwise I might—"

"What is going on here?" a shrill voice cut through the cafeteria from the front door. Miss Geeta was there, her mango-shaped body blocking the light. "What nonsense y'all carrying on with? This is why none of y'all can't pass no exams. Don't know anything in you books but you happy to skin your teeth and make joke whole day over nothing."

The students in the suddenly silent canteen were all looking at their toes, afraid to accidentally volunteer themselves for the teacher's attention. She pointed at Danesh. "I see that one there laughing with he jaw open big like a alligator, and don't care that he can't read two words in a row or that—" She loomed into the room theatrically. "Are you wearing a earring in school, boy?"

Instinct told Danesh his best chance was escape, so he started walking to the side door, while removing the stud.

"Don't turn your back on me!"

But he knew Miss Geeta wasn't going to treat him better for staying, so he kept moving. He waited out recess in the boy's washroom, though he wasn't surprised to find a summons to the principal's office waiting for him in his next class.

He fiddled with the stud in his pocket. This thing had been trouble from the start. His mother had forbidden him from buying it.

"You want to be a girl or what?" she had asked. "Man don't wear earring." She was so old fashioned. When Danesh wore it anyway, telling her that lots of boys wore studs, she had teased him about looking like a girl for a week, until his grandfather had come to his rescue. "Earring don't mean nothing," he said to his daughter-in-law with dismissive cheerfulness. "Look at all them old-time Bollywood movie star. Them man used to wear big earring pon all two ears and you can't tell me them was any girl. Them man had all them women crazy for them."

Danesh's mother had wavered a bit. Old Bollywood was one of her weaknesses. But she shook it off. "That don't matter. We ain't live in them time no more."

Danesh's grandfather – his *aja* – had simply followed with a gentle knockout argument, pointing at the line of framed deities on the narrow shelf of the living room wall. "And what about Ram and Krishna and Vishnu? All of them got earring. You gon' call them woman?"

His mother gritted her teeth and left. Danesh punched his *aja's* shoulder and they covered their laughter with their hands. His mother still scowled sometimes at his stud, but she never complained about it again.

He trudged up the stairs then along the empty corridor that lined the inside of the school courtyard.

Danesh preferred Bollywood movies, but his favourite movie in English was *Shawshank Redemption*, about a man wrongfully imprisoned for thirty years. He was not the kind to analyse things, but if he had, he would have realized that the movie was very much in the spirit of Bollywood: epic length, plot twists, despicable villains and most of all a pervading sense of justice delayed and denied, but ultimately achieved. It was only lacking the song and dance numbers.

Danesh didn't need to analyse anything to realize one fact, however – his school was built a lot like Shawshank prison. It was a rectangular ring of classroom blocks with a tarmac-covered yard in the middle where the students were expected to spend most of their free time. On Monday mornings, they held assembly in the shadowed half of the courtyard, next to a flag of Guyana that hung above everything from a steel flagpole.

The walls of the classrooms around the space were designed for airflow with vertical vents in the concrete. They reminded Danesh of the spaces between prison bars. There was a room number across the top of each door, like it really was a prison cell. The teachers were the guards, watching over the students like they were planning a riot.

Yes, this was Shawshank Secondary School.

And it was time to face the warden. He sat on the bench near the secretary, waiting his turn. Behind the door of the inner office, he could hear the principal, Miss Corrine, investigating a fight between two groups of boys.

Danesh wrinkled his nose. The dead whale's stink was definitely stronger now.

In the corridor outside the office door, one of the women who cleaned the school was complaining to her colleague about the office clerks who had called them to wipe up a spill even though the office had a mop of its own. "Is disrespect and eye-pass for we in this place. Like they too good fo' do real work." The women left without touching the puddle.

The boys who'd been in the brawl exited the inner door, their faces blank. Miss Geeta called Danesh in and made him stand before Miss Corrine's desk, the one with the varnish all rubbed away near the bottom edges. To the principal's left was Sir Karan, one of the younger teachers on staff and old Sir Carl, the deputy principal.

Four against one. Seemed fair. He wasn't worried though. It wasn't like they could beat him anymore. His *aja* had taken care of that too, at the start of the year.

That had been another day of suppressed giggles for Danesh, right here in the office with the principal and Miss Geeta.

Aja was the traditional Hindi word for 'father's father'. Danesh's *aja* was sixty-four, with hair that had gone grey at the sides. He refused to dye it, but he did keep it styled the old-fashioned way, with coconut oil and a slim, black comb. He was always shaved clean to his firm jaw and kept the top two buttons of his shirt open at all times because, as he put it, 'girls like fo' see chest hair'.

Danesh wasn't so sure about that last part. Even the Bollywood heroes seemed to shave their chests these days. But his grandfather wasn't doing too bad at romance. His wife had died ten years before and he had declared her the only woman worthy of being his wife, so he refused to re-marry. He was now a notorious 'sweet man,' visiting wives while their husbands were at work – and fighting off those husbands when they found out about his visitations, usually after the men fueled up with a few hours in the rum shop.

Aja was therefore no stranger to the lock-ups for his frequent squabbles, but all the policemen were his friends and as long as he took the arresting officers out for a few beers, no charges were ever filed. Of course, not even police friends could save you from a knife or cutlass, and *Aja* had a few belly scars to testify to his reflexes and good luck.

So the old man had not been intimidated when the Head Teacher had thrown on her best English and said, "Mr. Seeram, contrary to popular belief, the laws of this nation has not outlaw corporal punishment. It is a valuable tool regarding to the discipline of–"

"Listen, lady," *Aja* had said, waving his hand in annoyance, "The regulation say that any student get beat in school, it got fo' record in a punishment book and only a senior teacher can put the licks pon the child. So let anybody touch me grandson and I gon' come here first thing to see where in the book he name write and if you had proper cause. Don't play with me. I's a old lawyer-man from long now."

He pointed at Miss Geeta. "And let this witch behave she self. She done threated fo' beat Danesh and I know she still ain't get no promotion fo' be senior teacher. I gon' drive the police here to you front door pon me tractor fender if that's what it take, and get she lock up for child abuse."

Miss Geeta had been circumspect these last few months, but she still had it in for Danesh.

The inquisition in the case of the ear stud began with her laying out the tale of Danesh's evil disregard for manners and rules, ending with the teacher saying, "These children nowadays just don't care fo' they own self. And is we the teachers that get the blame. We can't let this behaviour stand."

Years in this system had taught Danesh that the fastest way out of any bad situation was silence. Speaking ran the risk of upsetting the adults. So, he just let his mind be as blank as his face and offered no defense.

Sir Carl wanted to suspend Danesh for two days. Miss Geeta thought a caning was called for. Sir Karan stayed silent – being just two years removed from his own time as a student, he was one of the few teachers that didn't have it in for the children he taught and actually spent time getting to know them.

The Head Teacher called a break in the trial when her phone went off. "Excuse me everyone, I has to take this. It's the Regional Education Officer."

What Miss Corrine had clearly expected to be a brief, business-like conversation, rapidly turned bad. From this side, all Danesh could hear was the principal being interrupted by an angry voice as she said things like, "But we never received–" and "I can assure you that if I had–"

For the first time since she had started this job a year ago, Danesh felt sympathy for her. Sure, she had been the one to create the plantain chip shortage by banning students from visiting the street vendors because of 'misbehaviour', but as Danesh watched her hold her temple and try to bargain her way out of whatever trouble she was in, she seemed defeated by life. The conversation ended with a contrite Miss Corrine saying, "Yes, sir ... Yes, sir ... Yes, sir."

As soon as she put down the phone, Miss Corrine lost his sympathy, however, because she shouted for her secretary and promptly began verbally hammering the girl. "Why you didn't give me the project forms that the office send since January? I look like a big dunce now in front of the officer, because I giving him out of date forms with the wrong information. You supposed to be keeping track of these things and you – you incompetent!"

The secretary took deep breaths and told her, "Ma'am, the documents I would have been given are the documents I would have handed over." It sounded to Danesh like she was trying to twist her lips until they magically squeezed out an answer that would get her out of trouble. It didn't work.

"Don't give me useless excuses," Miss Corrine said angrily.

The secretary stayed silent as the tirade continued for another minute, then she left to find the errant papers.

The principal turned her focus to Danesh. "You will write an apology letter."

Miss Geeta laughed sarcastically at the idea of him writing. Danesh smiled inside anyway. He could get Nadira to do it for him.

Sir Carl demanded a sterner punishment, but the Head Teacher waved him off, a tired look in her eyes.

"At least take the earring from him," he said.

The lie floated off Danesh's lips before he could even think. "I ain't got it, sir. It fall in the toilet bowl."

Miss Geeta took a step closer to Danesh. "So if we search you we won't find nothing?"

Again, Danesh thought of prison movies – and all the places guards would check for smuggled items. He handed over his stud, head down. Why hadn't he hidden the earring? His grandfather would have known to do that.

As he turned the corner after leaving the office, Danesh found Miss Corrine's secretary escorting the two cleaners back to the neglected spill. As the two women passed him with glum faces, he heard the secretary's voice chastising them like a fading police siren. "Y'all just lazy. Look how I got fo' bring you all the way up here and make sure you do you job..."

"You gon' write it for me?" Danesh asked. "You know you the best fo' this kinda thing."

It was lunchtime and only a few of Nadira's friends were in the classroom, sitting haphazardly in their mismatched furniture. He was standing next to her as he pleaded his case. By pretending he was after a *stylish* letter, Danesh hoped to avoid drawing attention to the fact that he couldn't write any letter at all. Normally, he would feel no shame about his illiteracy – a quarter of the new 7th grade students got sent to remedial English in this place. And another quarter probably needed it. But Nadira really was good. In fact, she used to write poetry when she was younger. Danesh had never read her poems – couldn't read them

THE DARK OF THE SEA | IMAM BAKSH

— but he was still impressed enough by the accomplishment to feel a vague guilt in her presence.

She smirked at the blank paper he was holding out and said to her friend, Alana, "Well, we know *he* not the best. Because, so Miss Geeta say. Is a good thing he give me plantain so I feel sorry for he." Her teasing was getting to him and the rising noise out in the courtyard was derailing his thoughts.

"Just make sure it done by time school over."

He dropped the sheet on the desk and walked away, ignoring her as she shouted, "Hey, don't make demand. Is you begging..."

There was a football game going in the courtyard. The sun had broken through the clouds to illuminate the wet tarmac and two full teams of eleven were kicking at the ragged black and white ball. They used two concrete pillars at each end to mark the goals. Most of the other students were standing in the shaded walkway that ringed the exercise area, cheering on the players. Even Amit's girlfriend, Susie, was watching, taking a break from her usual exile near the teacher's desk to brave the threat of sunlight darkening her skin. Danesh had never come close to being a football player, so he only ever watched.

There was more energy than skill on display in the middle. Often the ball would fly out of bounds through the spectators where it hit the outside of the classroom walls and rebounded into play.

Poor ball ain't got no way out.

Except for one moment. The biggest player on the field, a boy from the inland lake area named Kevitt, who played barefoot even on the rough tarmac, got so frustrated with his teammates not finding space that he blasted a shot the full length of the field. The ball soared toward the clouds in the sky.

An image drifted before Danesh's eyes. Two men on a

white sand beach with the dream-blue Pacific Ocean on their left. It was a scene of freedom from *Shawshank Redemption*. He could tell from the trajectory that the ball had the speed to make it over the classroom block and maybe even past the school's chain link outer fence.

Then a harsh clang broke the spell. The impact of the ball made the heavy Guyana flag shrug then it went back to hanging limply. The ball fell to Earth with a flat echo and the game resumed.

With ten minutes to go until the end of lunch, the players went to a penalty shootout. Danesh stood on the walkway just to the left of the goal, holding his breath with the other students crowded around for a closer look. Robot was nominated to be goalkeeper for his team and he used his spidery legs to deflect a tricky shot away from the corner of the goal. The next two shots missed high and then the other goalkeeper made a heroic stop, diving to the ground and coming up with scraped elbows.

Kevitt lined up his shot next. From the upstairs railing looking out over the courtyard, Nadira shouted at Robot, "You better duck this one or you gon' lose you head."

"If is one thing I can do in this life is take a knock," Robot shouted back. "I ain't frighten."

Danesh knew the first part to be true. He'd seen Robot's father punch and slap him a few times over the years. But he also knew there was a reason Robot didn't spend much time at home – he was definitely scared of being hit.

Kevitt wiped the sweat from his forehead. With his hair spiked into a quasi-mohawk and his nose flaring with each breath, he looked like a gladiator. After a run of three steps, he slapped the ball with the inside of his foot and it exploded at the goal. To be fair to Robot, while he did duck, he got his hands in the ball's path.

But all that did was deflect the ball right at Danesh. It hit him in the gut like a comet and all the world went silent.

Air didn't exist. At least there was none in his lungs anymore and none when he tried to breathe. He stood there, mouth open, eyes staring while the crowd watched in shock and amusement. He folded over in slow motion then dropped to his knees and vomited a yellow-white arc of sour food and slime.

Laughter. Everyone was laughing. Robot, Nadira, Susie ... Only Kevitt had the presence to come over and grab him around the chest, holding him upright.

His vision had gone blurry and every sound sent him off-balance. But one thing was clearly visible from his vantage point on the ground – there was a big toad sitting in the drain that led away from the courtyard. As Robot and Kevitt helped him up, the toad turned and hopped away, splashing the water as it went.

Danesh kept his head down all afternoon until it was time to collect his letter.

"I make the writing look scratchy," Nadira told him, handing over the folded paper. "Plus I spell every other word wrong, so they gon' think you write it."

"Anybody ever tell you that you mouth only full with–" He caught sight of a second letter in her hand and asked, "What's that?"

The ever-present Alana whispered in Nadira's ear and they giggled. Nadira said, "I decide that since you writing love letter to teacher, I gon' write one too."

"This is not no – wait, who you writing to?"

"Sir Karan," said Alana.

Nadira added, "I asking he if he got any vacancy in he love life because I available."

The idea of a teacher romantically involved with a student was of course scandalous, and Danesh was technically aware that it was illicit, but that sort of thing happened so often that he was more upset at the thought that Nadira wasn't checking to see if *he* had any vacancies. He said, "Karan? But he ears stick out and he nose like a bat."

"At least he can read the message I sending he."

John Cena, whose motto was, 'Don't ever give up,' was Danesh's favourite TV wrestler, but Nadira's insult hurt worse than a suplex off the top rope, so he decided 'Don't ever give up,' was just for TV. He left without another word. After dropping his apology at the school office, he headed home through the thickening miasma of rotting whale.

Danesh didn't bother changing out of his school uniform, though he did toss aside his sneakers for his imitation Clarks rubber sandals. From behind his bed, he extracted a small paper bag and put it in one pocket after making sure its conents were still there. He got his grandfather's old grass knife from its usual place on the wall near the kitchen door and left for the backdam on his bicycle.

The weapon felt potent in his hand. Except it wasn't a weapon, Danesh knew. He had seen a picture of it in his agriculture textbook once and the word underneath had intrigued him enough that he had spent a minute to decipher 'sickle'. It was a good name. It was one of the few words that stuck in his head, except he saw it as 'SICKle' because it was a sick blade: the four-inch handle held a tapered steel curve that resembled a new moon. The inside of the blade was notched with dozens of jagged little teeth that could slice anything open.

He remembered the first time he had truly proven its power. A Peace Corps teacher named Miss Emmasyn had arrived a few years before. She had explained to Danesh that he probably had something called 'dyslexia' and that he could beat it. "It takes effort," she said, smiling with a big hardcover book in her hand. "Now, I know you love stories. I always hear you telling the children about the latest Bollywood movie you saw or some of those epic legends from your temple. That's why I borrowed this from the library in Affiance." She showed him the painting on the front, a battle scene with the four-armed god, Vishnu. "It's illustrated so you can follow the stories and that way you'll be able to develop your decoding skills."

Real hope had burned in his 12-year-old heart that night when he took the book home. Knowing the name of the thing in his head that had made him stupid all these years meant he could kill it.

Except he couldn't read even the few words required in the picture book. When he looked at the text it was like he could only see the shapes of the blank spaces between the letters. Or sometimes like the letters were playing hide-and-seek behind each other. The pictures didn't help. In fact, they made things worse because the lush colours and dramatic poses only taunted him with the stories he was missing.

He threw the book down. Vishnu seemed to mock him from the cover and Danesh's anger boiled. He took down the SICKle. Its shape prevented him from slashing across the god's picture, so he began carving away the cover at its outsides. The feel of that cardboard suffering under his hand had thrilled him, and Danesh had not stopped until the whole book was shredded.

Later, he told Miss Emmasyn that he had lost the book, but he wasn't a good enough liar to make her believe that. She was back in America these days, but Danesh still thought of the hurt look on her face sometimes.

Danesh rode into the backdam – the inland rice farming area – past the sandy stretch of ground that everyone simply called, 'The Sand,' and found a good patch of wild antelope grass. Thanks to the sickle, he quickly filled his sack.

Next, a stop in The Sand, at *Aja's* fruit and vegetable farm. His grandfather had never spoken to Danesh about the ganja he grew there, hidden behind the tomatoes and ochroes, but the boy was sure *Aja* knew he sometimes picked a few buds for himself. His current supply of dried weed was down to just the little bit in the paper bag, so he stocked up.

Another half minute of riding got him to *Aja's* house, where he checked on the two cows currently in the shed. Even though his grandfather lived some distance from the sea, the stink of the whale was drifting in. And it wasn't a healthy stink like the cow pies that covered his grandfather's backyard, but a malignant invasion of the nostrils.

Luckily, the place where all the fishing boats were parked on the beach was a quarter-mile upwind from the whale. Amit was sitting with two other village boys in a boat that had been pulled high up on the sloping brown sand. Robot was with them. He lived five villages away, but he rarely went home before dark. They were playing dominoes.

"Watch this smart man," Robot told the others, pointing at Danesh. "Bring grass knife to the beach. You going and cut some sand fo' you cow?"

The other boys laughed, but Danesh didn't care. He left the knife hanging on its cord over the bike handlebar and reached for the ganja in his pocket.

"Don't come here," Amit joked, slapping the side of the boat when Danesh reached it. "The game full. Four man done sit down."

Danesh pulled his hand back empty. Fine. No weed for them. This wasn't where he really wanted to be anyway. He turned to the grey ocean and spotted his boat at the shoreline. Danesh smiled, pushed his butt back at the other boys and let rip a fart. He had long mastered the technique to make it rumble with a pleasing 'brrrrmmmm'.

The four boys leapt out of the boat as if a bomb had gone off, cursing at him and spitting sand as they rose up. Danesh sprinted away before they thought to hold him down and get revenge. He took the sickle as he passed the bike.

As he untied his boat a minute later, Amit walked over. "You want some company? I know you got something good in you pocket."

"I want cruise by me self a li'l bit," Danesh said, keeping his voice friendly.

"You don't ever get worried out there by you'self? I mean,

they got people thiefing engine and throwing people overboard."

"Nobody don't want *this*," said Danesh pointing at the dented cover of his undersized 15 horsepower outboard.

"Don't forget black magic," Amit warned. "They does sacrifice li'l boy out here you know."

"That only happen one time. Long time ago."

"Fifteen years not that long," said Amit, raising a teasing eyebrow, "They might ready to go again."

The engine whined and coughed as Danesh headed south through the wide passage between Tiger Island and the coast. He had tossed his shirt onto the floorboards and was warm even in the overcast weather as he took the sun on his bare shoulders and feet. The wind blew his hair back from his forehead. Maybe he should grow it out like Shah Rukh Khan in *Asoka*. Man, Shah Rukh had been the boss in that movie. Well, except for the end when he decided to give up being a warrior.

Danesh passed by the grey bulk of the whale and even out here there was a whiff of decay. Unlike this morning, the rocky shore was clear of people.

Danesh and his sputtering engine sailed the length of the island. The twenty-foot boat had once been an abandoned wreck, but Amit had helped him seal the cracks and holes with fresh lumber and tar. The bottom still leaked a bit, but it was good for an afternoon of running about.

He made it to his objective, the buoy that marked the river channel for the ferry. This spot south of Tiger Island was where he and his friends often spent a couple of hours jumping into the water, free from the world. Lately, Danesh had become fascinated with the new reflector mounted on the floating marker. Sunlight would split into the colours of a rainbow when it struck the plastic plate and Danesh found it hypnotic. Today he was going to steal it.

He tied his boat to the buoy and put the grass knife to work right away, prying at the plastic. The reflector snapped off without any trouble and Danesh stared at it as he sat near the engine. Light seemed to have been sprinkled across the smooth surface in red, gold, blue, and green. The illusion calmed him and he opened the throttle.

He put his prize down so he could concentrate as he moved east. The constant battle between the river mouth's channels and the incoming tides kept shifting the sands around here. Each low tide seemed to reveal a different network of lagoons and sandbars. With the water near low, like now, the unseen bottom could damage his propeller.

Once he was through the maze, however, he tossed the anchor and it hit bottom at the end of about ten feet of rope. He was at the edge of the open stretch between Tiger Island and the larger island of Wakenaam.

Curious, Danesh scratched away a bit of the coating from the reflector with the tip of his knife, revealing dull grey plastic underneath. He set the reflector down and dug out the ganja from his pocket.

A sense of alarm jolted through him. He gripped his knife tighter and snapped his head left and right, but the river seemed clear.

Then a dark, human-sized, shape burst up from the water and landed on the boat, rocking it. It snarled at Danesh in undecipherable words and swung a spear at him. The tip scratched his stomach, breaking the skin. Danesh tumbled backwards, falling into the water without ever getting a good look at the creature.

Then he was sinking. He needed to breathe! But there was no air. He was going to drown. Just like when the football had struck him, his lungs refused to work.

He recalled the football incident. *No, I gon' vomit and then drown. And I gon' probably drown pon me own vomit.*

It took him a few seconds to realize he wasn't going to die. Just like when he'd been knocked into the water years before, he could see everything clearly despite the thick brownness of the water. And he could breathe. Danesh looked at the knife in his hand. He had dropped the ganja, but he had kept hold of his sickle.

He...

He could see *her*. His clear sight showed him that the creature was a girl about his age and size. Even with the bottom of the boat between them, his Clearsight revealed her standing inside it. Her skin was blue-black, and scales coated her legs, right up to her waist. Her long hair was in a thick braid and it was silver – not white or grey, but literally the colour of fine metal.

At first, he thought she was wearing only a black tube top and short tights, plus a streamlined pouch strapped to each thigh. But a deeper look showed that there was also a clear coating over her skin, like a hard but flexible shell, that moved with her as she turned, scanning the water. Something about the lurching steps of her motion made Danesh think her mind was not working right.

The girl plunged into the water and when the bubbles cleared, she was floating upright with her back to him. Her feet had transformed into a long, almost snakelike, tail with a wide fin at the end. Gills were opening and closing erratically on either side of her neck.

Danesh had listened to enough of the old people's stories to recognize her as a *fe*maid, though Miss Emmasyn said the original pronunciation was 'fairmaid'. They were monsters in disguise, who were known to seduce men and murder them for sport. Although, this one apparently didn't care for the seduction stage of the process, judging by the burning cut near his navel.

The shock of his attack and immersion had worn off enough for Danesh to look for an escape. Tiger Island was behind him and he turned for it. He felt like he was flying, swimming five times as fast as he ever did before, even with the knife in one hand.

But the fairmaid had seen him now, and he could hear her high-pitched scream of rage through the water as she came for him, her spear leading the way. And she was swimming a lot faster than he could.

His only hope was the shallows. There would not be enough depth for her to whip the water with her tail there. For a moment, he considered dropping the knife to swim faster, but if he was caught, he would need the blade to fight. Danesh broke through the surface and made it to the wide top of an underwater sandbar. He took a gulping breath, then set his feet under him and kept running in the shin-deep water.

At first, the fairmaid tried to circle around him in the lagoon-like space alongside the finger of sand he was running on, but his trap had worked. She couldn't swim with speed in the shallow water. Leaving the lagoon, she switched to her legged form then ran after him on the sandbar, splashing water with each step. He smiled as he realized that she could not run fast enough. He sprinted even harder, opening up their separation. Then his smile vanished when he realized the sandbar did not run all the way to shore.

A hundred feet away was the forested shoreline, but the darkness of the water ahead revealed a depth that he would not be able to cross on foot.

Behind him, the fairmaid saw it too and she screeched in savage glee.

Under the water, Danesh had not needed to worry about breathing, but up here in the air, he panted and wheezed as he ran out of sand and started swimming through the last bit of deep water. He didn't look back as he heard the fairmaid splash into the water behind him. He tried to gauge how much of a lead he had, but the water muffled sounds too much for him to tell. Just as he crawled up onto the solid beach at the other side, the fairmaid vaulted from the water toward him. Time seemed to slow and he noted the way the light scattered in red, green, blue, and yellow as it passed through the fountaining spray of water around her before she landed on the sand. Time clicked back to normal as she jabbed at him with her weapon. He rolled sideways and kicked her ankle. She fell to her knees, crying out in pain and it seemed like she was too tired to get up. Danesh scrambled to his feet and ran inland.

In the cover of the trees, he turned. The fairmaid stood at the water's edge. She was clearly ill. Her eyes were red and swollen, lined with pulsing veins that seemed ready to pop. Her gills were leaking blood. She swayed then fell face-first into the sand.

He gripped the sickle tighter upon seeing how vulnerable she was and ran to her. He kicked aside the spear and lifted her head up and set his blade at her neck. The sickle seemed full of power, so much that it was overflowing into his arm.

The fairmaid reached a feeble arm up to grab his wrist and–. No, she was reaching for a jewelled pendant which hung around her neck on a beaded necklace. He waited, and eventually she squeezed it.

In the distance, under the sea, something flashed, visible in his Clearsight, but not to his normal eyes.

The fairmaid looked at him. Except for the dark blue skin, her features seemed very human. Not totally, though. With her hair back, he could see that the tips of her ears were pointed, like the corners of a butterfly wing.

She spoke, her voice harsh and full of wet air, in a language he did not understand. The skin of her throat brushed his hand. It was very warm. Feverish, even. She pointed in the direction of the flash he had seen earlier. There was a circle of swirling light there, about half a mile away, under the waves.

And this creature that had just tried to murder him wanted Danesh to take her there. To save her.

The sickle pulsed in his grip. But, looking down at the fairmaid, he felt his anger abating. He dropped the knife in the sand and that calmed him even more. He lifted her. She was heavy and unable to help support her own weight, so he stumbled with her into the water. Even after she transformed into her tailed form, however, she was still too weak to assist.

Not that it mattered. Moving through the water felt like flying now and his kicks sent him easily towards the swirling blueish light. He could probably swim all the way to Trinidad the way he was feeling. All the way to America even.

Close up, the circle was like the opening of a tunnel and

the fairmaid signalled that he should step in. He thought about just pushing her through but realized she might need his help on the other side. Danesh kicked at the water behind him and swam out of the world he had known.

The tunnel hummed with a deep 'ummmbb' and calmly opened on the other side. He was still in the ocean, but this was blue, like the Pacific in the movies. Fish of all sizes were darting and swirling in all directions, in every colour of the rainbow. Hundreds of feet below, thick vegetation swayed on the sun-dappled floor of the rocky surface.

A shadow fell upon him. Over the sea floor too. He panicked for an instant, then a friendly whistling call filtered down. A whale, larger than the one now dead on the beach back home, drifted over him, close enough for him to see every detail of the fluted lines that ran along its bulging underside. He watched, open-mouthed as it sailed ahead.

With his Clearsight, he looked through the haze of the sloping distance and saw the top of a city. There were people here! Living in towers and domes of crystal.

Some of those people were coming straight at him in fact. At the edge of the far city, he could make out five serious-faced women, each with the same dark skin as the fairmaid in his arms, but with hair of various hues from pink to blue. And all with bladed spears. They seemed to get angrier as they swam closer.

Time to go back. Even if they didn't try to kill him as soon as they reached him, he didn't know the words to explain why their friend was dying.

He yanked the pendant off of the fairmaid, then left her drifting in the sunlit water and swam back through the tunnel just as it started to collapse.

As soon as he was back in the muddy water of the Essequibo mouth, he began to wonder if he was going insane.

Had that really happened? He swam for shore, his superior speed and his Clearsight staying with him, though he could sense them weakening.

By the time he had recovered the sickle and the spear and got the motor started on his boat, he was ordinary old Danesh again.

He could barely walk into the house when he arrived just after sunset, his sore limbs telling him that he had not imagined his encounter with the fairmaid.

His father's work clothes were gone from the wash line near the backyard shower so Danesh knew he would be at work until morning. He checked that his mother was watching her Indian soaps and took the fairmaid's spear upstairs and laid it on his bed, unwrapping the rags he had used to disguise it when he walked home. The weapon was made of two halves. The top was a double-edged sword shape made of a pearly material and the bottom was a grip of grey bone, etched with a design that looked like leaves laid side-by-side. Or maybe they were fangs?

Danesh's clothes were still damp, so he stripped them off. He lifted up the pendant which looked like a drop of water. He touched it, expecting it to scatter like liquid, but it remained hard and smooth. He laid it on his dresser and looked for fresh underwear in his drawer.

Loud pounding at the door startled him. "Hey, boy," Amit shouted, "stop playing with you'self in there."

Danesh hid the spear in his wardrobe at the same time he was hopping on one foot, pulling on his briefs.

"Don't think I can't hear you," Amit laughed. "We don't got time for that now. People waiting pon you."

"What you doing here?" Danesh asked when he opened the door.

Amit took a seat on his bed. "We supposed fo' go the park, remember?"

"Oh." Danesh blocked Amit's view and picked up the pendant, placing it in his pocket.

"I just see you walk in with a big fish or something?" Amit asked, looking around.

Danesh harshly said, "I think you goin' blind."

Amit scowled. He had excellent eyesight and he knew it.

The park was a new seaside relaxation area attached to the Affiance community center. It was a space of neat grass and a half-dozen trees – with some slides and swings for the little children and concrete benches and tables for the grown-ups.

The real attraction for Danesh and his friends was the free wireless Internet provided by the library. They all had computers, but neither Danesh's nor Amit's family could afford Internet and Robot ... well, no one wanted to be at Robot's house in case his father came home.

Kevitt had joined them tonight. He was an anomaly at their school, a student who took his work seriously and did well. The only reason he hadn't passed the exam for the good high school was the poor quality of teaching back at the small Amerindian village where he grew up. Unlike them, he was at the park to do chemistry research, not hunt for porn.

But even he had to acknowledge priorities, so it was the x-rated videos that they went to first, sitting at a round table in the corner of the park where no one could see their screen.

Once he had snuck onto the network, Danesh let the others take over the epic quest and he looked around at the people under the bright lights.

The Strong Man wasn't here tonight. That was how Danesh thought of the supervisor of the gym that was part of the community centre. The Strong Man was about thirty and could often be seen near the front of the building in a vest that showed off his bulky physique. He was there during the day too, running the library.

Waves washed against the other side of the sea dam with a continuous hissing. Was it just two hours ago that he'd been attacked by a wild fish-tailed sea girl carrying a spear? That he'd visited a city under the ocean through a magic gate?

Could the doctors at the hospital fix his brain if he was

just imagining all this?

Around him people were doing ordinary things in an ordinary world. A mother was settling a quarrel over ice-cream between two toddlers. Three boys were seeing who could climb up a tree the fastest.

A white-robed Muslim man with a long beard was pushing his two-year-old in the baby swing, making coochi-coo noises. Watching the man play with his son with such care and joy reminded Danesh of when he had been little and his grandfather would sit him on a pillow over his bicycle's tow bar and ride with him around the village. And the whole time Danesh would talk cheerfully about everything that came to his young mind.

But it was a lie. The mental numbness that had kept him functional during the fighting and fleeing was wearing off. A rising panic quickened Danesh's heartbeat. These people needed to be warned. This ordinary world only looked peaceful and easy. There were monsters under the water. And the monsters were coming.

The robed man let his older son take over pushing the swing and sat on a nearby bench. He began singing in a way that sounded like praying. It was clearly verses of some sort and at the end of each section he would intone 'Ameen'. He let the *mmmmm* slide on his lips for long moments so that the sound had time to bounce between Danesh's ears, leaving a tingle of pleasure. His pulse fell and his breathing calmed. It was like he had returned to the bench in the park after falling in an endless darkness.

The other boys were still sampling their illicit videos, arguing over which ones Danesh should download for them.

"Alright, nobody move." It was the Strong Man walking up to their table. Robot made a break for it and the man caught him by the arm and sat him down hard.

"Who's you?" Kevitt demanded. Danesh could tell he was

scared underneath though. He had very religious parents.

The man looked them over with a clenched jaw. "My name is Mr. Jones and you on my network. Nobody going anywhere 'til y'all explain how you get past my security and disguise the machine ID."

Danesh sat in silence with the others.

Amit remembered to close the lid of the computer, for whatever innocence that bought them. "If you say somebody disguise they self fo' thief porn from you, then you can't know is we do it."

Jones laughed. "I see four teenagers hiding they screen and giggling. Who else it gon' be? Now tell me who do the breaking and entering or I gon' call the police."

"It was he," said Robot, pointing at Danesh.

"How you sell you friend out like that?" asked Amit.

"Is Danesh sit down direct in front anyway. You think the man don't know?"

As the other two bickered, Jones smiled at Danesh. "Show me what you do,"

So Danesh did. Halfway through his explanation the man laughed. "I feel stupid I didn't guard against this now. I just never expect somebody to do all that work. How you figure it out though? You learn networking in school?"

"No. I just kind of read the online help about the network tools and kind of see the best way to connect it up."

Jones looked at Danesh's face, doubtful. "Well, you might got some talent for this work. If you want, you can come around to the library and I can teach you 'bout it. The real way, not this by-guess thing you doing."

The library? Danesh thought of all those books in there – waiting to attack him. "Umm, is alright," he said. "I not really interested in computer stuff."

"If you say so, boss." The man walked away across the grass.

Danesh called after him, "What about the gym?"

"You looking to get fit?"

"I want get strong. You can show me?"

Danesh expected ridicule at this point, maybe a joke about how hopeless his skinny arms were. Instead, the big man just smiled. "We open 'til eight every night." Then he went into the library.

Five minutes later the other boys groaned as their videos stopped loading.

Riding their bikes home, just the two of them, Amit asked Danesh, "How come you want lift weights all of a sudden?"

"Just a feeling. Like things happening in the world and I got fo' prepare."

Amit grinned, "Or you planning to fight Miss Geeta?"

Sunday mornings, Danesh went to the temple for stories. His *Aja* had long since explained to him the ins and outs of the pandit game, so he didn't take the religion part seriously.

But Ram and Sita and Latchmi and Kali and Vishnu. Demons and ogres and weapons made of lightning. Battles that levelled mountains! Not to mention the clean, clear beat on the dolak drum in-between the spoken parts of the stories.

But that Sunday, six days after meeting the fairmaid, he limped out of the service wondering how much truth there might be in the old tales. It had been in the form of a half-fish that Vishnu had rescued the first man from a flood, so it wasn't crazy that Danesh should meet a half-fish girl, was it?

His thighs and calves were in pain. His necks and arms too. Two gym sessions this week had devastated him. Maybe he should skip the workout today?

No. He wrinkled his nose at the smell of the rotting whale and got on his bike. The mysterious sense of purpose that had struck him the night after the fairmaid attack still drove him.

But being motivated didn't mean he couldn't complain. As Jones started the session an hour later, Danesh said, "I can barely lift me hand."

"Yeah, they call that DOMS."

"Yeah, 'dumbs' is right. I must be dumb fo' let you do this to me."

"D-O-M-S. It mean delayed onset muscle soreness – I hope you ain't think that this gon' be easy?"

"No, but it better work."

"You see this?" said Jones, curling his arm to display a large, well-toned bicep. "This take me five years. You gon' be a bony li'l boy for a long time no matter how much pain you put you'self through."

Danesh looked at the iron weights on the squat rack. "So, what's the point then?"

"The point is you got to start some time or you don't get nowhere in the end."

Danesh thought of something the old man from *Shawshank Redemption* had said – that you had to either get on with living or get on with dying. He got in position under the bar and took a breath. Time for him to get on with *lifting*.

· · 🐂 · ·

In the afternoon, he found Amit at work in the backdam. He was filling the canister of a backpack sprayer with water and herbicide. Surwa was there since he didn't get along with Amit's parents.

Around them were brown fields awaiting planting. Most had been flooded by water from the lakes and now tall, white cranes stalked fish in the shallow, muddy water.

As Amit finished the delicate procedure, Danesh rubbed Surwa's belly. He had never had a dog of his own because his grandfather was allergic. "Make sure you wash you hand good," he told Amit when he'd closed the cap on the spray can. "Otherwise you might get it in you mouth by accident and suicide you'self."

Amit gave him an annoyed glance then climbed down the sloped side of the dirt road to the drainage trench and washed his hands in the murky water.

Amit strapped on the pack but sat back down instead of setting off into the field. They were under an old *gama* tree, one that was practically an old friend. Every Easter, he and Amit would pick the green berries and use their sticky pap to glue their kites together.

Danesh still felt guilty over lying to Amit about the spear. The spear ... That was real. It was proof that he wasn't crazy. He put a hand in his pocket and played with the jewel there. That was real too. He looked at his friend and wondered if he would believe him about a fairmaid.

"Amit..."

"What?"

No. He couldn't tell. Amit would think he was cracked in the head.

Amit waved a hand in front of Danesh. "What?"

"Um, that thing you did talking 'bout before. The black magic killing?"

"Yeah."

"Was my uncle do it."

"What!? Serious? You uncle Janak? The one who hang he self?"

"Yeah." Danesh rubbed the dog's ears, wondering how much of insanity was from a person's family blood. "The case never went to trial, but he admit he kidnap the boy and sacrifice he for blessings or some craziness like that. *Aja* say the man just run mad one day with no warning, start talking different language and so."

"You mean like Spanish or Hindi?"

"No, like nonsense."

"A fake language?" Amit asked.

"I don't know. *Aja* only talk about it one time when he did drunk."

"Oh," Amit stood and tested the balance of the poison on his back. "So why you telling me this?"

Danesh remembered the look of hurt and suspicion on Amit's face when he had made fun of him the night after he was attacked. "Well, we's friend and friend don't keep secret, right?"

I have a fish-girl's spear in my bedroom! The words bounced around his skull, but he still couldn't get them out his mouth.

"Well," Amit said, "As long as we talking honest, I um, well, Susie–"

A deep, happy voice floated in from the west, singing a chirpy line in Hindi.

Danesh jumped to his feet, cupped his hands around his mouth and answered with the next line of the song. He didn't know the meaning of the words, but he made sure to sing the line a little faster, just as he had memorised from years of listening to it on the TV.

His grandfather was approaching, riding his old bicycle along the pale dirt road while leading a pregnant cow past a line of coconut trees. He and Danesh sang lines of the old movie song as the distance closed, making sure to leave out the slower parts. This had been what they sang on bike rides when Danesh had been young feeling like he was in his own Bollywood movie.

"What the two y'all doing out here by you'self?" the old man asked. Surwa the dog had learned as a pup to stay away from Danesh's *aja* so he was sitting some distance away, growling resentfully.

Before Danesh could retort, *Aja* turned to Amit. "You alright? I hear you get some bad news?"

Danesh looked at his friend. "What bad news?"

Amit looked sheepish. "Susie parents sending she away to Georgetown. They arranging for she marry a university boy from New York."

"But she only sixteen."

"That's why they sending she to town fo' wait 'til she reach age and the boy graduate."

Danesh asked, "So what you gon' do?"

"I could find carpenter work in Georgetown. I know how–"

"Listen, boy," said *Aja*. "You got fo' use you head, okay? Don't tie up you future pon one woman. Life full of chance. Look at me. I lost me wife and people start criticise 'bout how I having girlfriend right away and like I don't care, but Danesh can tell you, I love me wife."

Danesh nodded. Even his mother talked about how strong *Aja's* devotion to his wife, Meena, had been.

His grandfather squeezed Amit's shoulder, "But life for who doing the living. You can't say you lost something and go make bad decision. You young. Enjoy it."

Amit nodded, eyes down.

Then *Aja* looked at Danesh. "As for you, I want you look at this cow good. You gon' got fo' look after it by you'self fo' me."

"Alright," said Danesh, without hesitation. "But why?"

"I leaving for the diamond bush in another two weeks."

"You goin' and dig fo' diamond?" Amit asked.

"No, the real money in them mining area is selling. Food, liquor, whore ... one thing don't ever change is man got to eat, drink and–"

"What about the farm, *Aja*?"

"You leave me farm alone. Especially the section at the back." He smiled and pointed to the old stone tomb just visible through the trees. "The Dutch Man gon' guard that fo' me."

The boys laughed, but they knew it was a good plan. Even they feared the old ghost reputed to haunt the spot.

"People easy fo' trick," said *Aja*. "Like when I been in

the diamond bush before I get married. I used fo' got this friend would bring in them young ladies to me rum shop. After he order he two beer, I would lean over and talk in he ears, loud enough for she hear and say, 'Hey man, you know, that diamond you show me, I can only give you a two thousand US for it. If you carry it to Georgetown you can get four, but I can only give you two. Maybe two and a half.'"

Aja chuckled at the memory and continued, "And the village girl would hear me say 'US money' and she done make up she mind she going home with he tonight."

"But what you get out of that, *Aja*? He pay you?"

"No. But he owe me a favour for later. That's how you get through life – favour and sweet talk."

As his grandfather rode off, the old man began singing *Tumko Hamari*. The song had been performed by a woman in the movie, *Ayee Milan Ke Bela*, but *Aja's* deep voice gave it a dramatic weight that worked well. In fact, he often boasted that it was singing that song which had won over Meena when they had been 'courting'. "Plus, I look just like Rajendra Kumar in me young days," *Aja* would always add with a wink, referring to the movie's star.

Danesh turned back to Amit. "You really going to George–"

But his friend was already across the logs that bridged the drainage trench, his back bent under the weight of the spray can. For a moment, Amit seemed like an old man and Danesh wanted to run after him and keep him from walking into the rice field, but what could he say? Amit's mind was made up. He was going to Georgetown and the unravelling of their friendship that had started when he dropped out of school was going to be complete.

Danesh kicked at a chunk of dry dirt and turned for home.

Sometime past midnight, Danesh awoke as several strong hands yanked him out of bed. They held him upright and before he was fully in his senses one of the people restraining him clamped a hand over his mouth and nose. In the dark, he sensed that there were at least six or seven people in his bedroom. He tried to move, but the strength of his captors was too much to even wriggle.

"Where you have it?" asked a calm but threatening voice. A girl's voice. For an instant, Danesh was alarmed to realize he was wearing only briefs, but he forgot about that when the voice spoke again, slowly and with restrained anger. "Where you hide me *daki*?"

He tried to ask what a *daki* was but could only emit a muffled plea that exhausted his lungs. He tried to breathe in more air, but the hand over his face prevented him inhaling much. What he got was a smell like saltwater.

Behind him, another voice spoke, a high-pitched, chittering sound that was not English.

"Is him for sure," said the girl-voice. Then the dark face loomed into his vision, her eyes bright and clear and her braided silver hair just visible in the starlight coming through the window.

If Danesh saving her life had earned him any sympathy, the fairmaid did not show it. "Tell me," she said with cold insistence. "Unless you want you neck break."

Danesh turned his eyes to the wardrobe where he had left the spear. The silver-haired girl checked the door as if it could be booby-trapped and then retrieved her *daki*. She looked it over and nodded to whoever was holding Danesh.

He sagged in relief. Good. They could take the girl and the *daki* and all the other craziness and go and leave him alone.

But the hands holding him only got tighter. He was still struggling to breathe, and his head was getting dizzy. Again, the weird voice spoke from behind him. Then another like it.

"He not gon' need no clothes," the girl said to them. "Just bring he fast, before anybody come."

Danesh screamed against the muffling hand. Being kidnapped was bad enough, but half-naked too?

Another question from the strong person behind him.

Silverhair said, "Last time he could breathe in the water. I ain't know how, but the Mark of Zadoq'ua must be have something to do with it."

Danesh's second-floor room had old casement windows of frosted glass and wood. He had left them open as usual and the space between the two opened panels was large enough to allow people to pass through. As his captors led him over to the window, he saw some of the others in the room. They were all fairmaids, with the gleaming blue-black skin that seemed to fold them into the darkness. All of them held weapons – mostly *dakis*, but also some knives and scissor-looking things. None of them had the first fairmaid's distinctive silver hair, however, and they seemed older and stronger too.

Hanging over the window sill was a length of thin rope-like material that was smooth and spongy. It was held on the inside of his window by a bonelike hook.

One strong fairmaid took him from the others with one

arm and held the rope as she climbed outside. Danesh held on tight, as she lowered herself with the skill of a monkey. He tried to break free the minute she touched the ground, but she had the presence of mind to keep his feet in the air and two more fairmaids soon dropped at his side and held him still.

Silverhair dropped down too. "Let me tie he hand before he try something." She reached to one of the pouches at her hip. On her wrist, a wide, silver bangle etched with seahorses flashed as it caught the light from a streetlamp. From within the pouch, she removed a thin, short piece of the sponge-rope with metal knobs at either end. The rope felt uncomfortably warm and smooth as she fit it around his wrists behind his back. Then the sponge-rope tightened around him, compressing like a constrictor snake.

"Please, you can't do this," Danesh said to Silverhair, his guardian having forgotten to cover his mouth after the descent. "I ain't know if I can make myself breathe under the water again. I need me hand fo' swim and–"

Silverhair fished out an identical piece of sponge rope and set it in his mouth before wrapping it around his head to make a gag. Again it squeezed tight, making Danesh unable to speak. The warm, stone-like taste of it made him want to cough.

One of the older fairmaids asked a question and Silverhair replied, "He ain't saying nothing important."

One fairmaid carried him easily now that he was bound. She had him draped upside-down on her shoulders with his head near her naked belly. No, not naked. All the fairmaids had that transparent coating over their bodies. He could feel it whenever her walking caused his cheek to swing against her skin. It reminded him of the gel coating on medicine capsules, solid but flexible. He tried to lean his body away so the fairmaid wouldn't get offended.

She didn't seem to care. The whole group moved quietly

and methodically in the night, up the unlit side street and past the dark houses. Over in Clarendon's house a TV was glowing, but no one was moving. Some of the old seawall still stood here with its sections of chipped and weathered cement work. They climbed over in silent coordination and dropped into the calm, waist-deep water.

Each fairmaid gave a quick look around to make sure nothing was amiss and then they leapt forward in unison. Danesh caught a glimpse of scaly, fish-like tails flashing and then it was dark.

He panicked as his Clearsight refused to kick in.

I gon' drown. Oh God, I gon' drown!

Then he realized he wasn't suffocating. But why couldn't he see? The answer made him embarrassed: in his fright, he had shut his eyes tight. Now he opened them. The water was cool against his eyes and he could see everything. It was somewhat darker than when he had been attacked by Silverhair, but that was the only difference in the night time ocean. He could see almost as far and see just as many details. The muddy surface of the descending seafloor, the little crabs hiding within, the fish hunting for them industriously with their heads down, the shrimp drifting by ... he saw it all as his captor dragged him along by an elbow.

It was a long swim and became boring as the view didn't change for some time. Danesh watched Silverhair and the others, but all they did was swim with flowing lashes of their tails, looking around alertly and keeping to a staggered formation.

The sea bottom became more sandy. The water less salty. They were swimming towards the river mouth. A dull circle appeared ahead and grew into a hole that Danesh recognized – the gateway to the undersea city.

The squad of fairmaids entered one at a time, Danesh

going fifth. The brief darkness of the tunnel almost made him panic, but the deep 'ummbbh' sound relaxed him and he emerged into a twilight sea. It was not the same bright blue as before. The muted colours and softer reflections made it seem dreamlike and calm.

Danesh found himself relaxing. Not just from the environment, but now that he was through the portal, he accepted that this was really happening. Ahead, the city loomed larger. It was made of cylindrical towers constructed with intricate glassy walls that widened and tapered in flowing lines. Some towers were symmetrical, others spiraling and yet others seeming to change even as he looked at them. The only common feature was that each building was capped with a dome as wide as its base.

They swam into the midst of the towers and Danesh stared up. They were hundreds of feet tall, like skyscrapers. He could see through the clear walls that inside the buildings were dry and the people were walking. None of them carried weapons, he noted. Everyone had the same blue-black skin as the squad of soldiers who had captured him. Their hair colours varied wildly, however, as did the hairstyles. Everything from afros to waist length curtains.

Most people wore robes, though some were naked – or close to it. With only transparent walls, he figured these people didn't care much for privacy. Almost all of them seemed to be women, but a few were unmistakably men.

That reminded Danesh to look down and make sure his briefs were on properly. They were, but being wet, they were a lot more translucent than he would have liked. There was nothing he could do about it, however, as he was dragged along, his shoulder aching.

There were no streets, forcing the group to take a winding path, but the buildings were spread well apart from each other, allowing the free movement of fairmaids and wildlife. The shadowed ground between buildings was full of coral reefs – with fish and turtles and seaweed and other crawly and floaty things he couldn't name filling the spaces. One dolphin swam close to Danesh and looked him over while spiraling up and around and under him. The beast was actually intimidating in its size, being a lot larger up close than they seemed on TV shows. The dolphin twittered excitedly and four more came over, noisily joining the escort.

Over to Danesh's left one of the many fairmaids in the open water swam to the wall of a seascraper. She put her hand out and just *melted* through to the inside. Or rather, the wall appeared to let her push right through it so that she emerged standing on her two legs, her skin and hair dry.

The procession continued to the tallest seascraper, in the centre of the city. When they reached the base, the fairmaids thrashed the water with their tails and swam straight up at a pace that made Danesh grit his teeth.

By the time the upward swim ended, he could see a city below him that covered miles in every direction.

How come nobody ever find this place? All these years, some submarine or diver must–

He was jerked right through the wall. From the feel of it against his skin, it seemed similar to the gel coating the fairmaids were wearing. And it had absorbed all the water from his skin, he realised.

The soldiers – that's what they had to be – took no time for adjusting to having feet instead of tails and immediately marched him down a clear-walled corridor. In fact, the floor and high ceiling were clear too. For the most part, light reflected and bent by the many layers of the walls made it impossible to see far, yet there was a feeling of being in an airy and open space.

That feeling ended when the squad marched him through the gel wall at the end of the corridor and he found himself in a fully mirrored room, devoid of any fixtures. He was in their version of a jail cell, he assumed.

They chucked him at the wall, and he collided with its cushioned surface just hard enough to knock him off-balance, and he fell to the cool floor.

Silverhair grabbed his neck in a careful, but firm, motion and pulled him to his feet, freeing his sponge-rope gag, "Time fo' you talk. Tell me why I can feel Zadoq'ua in you."

"I don't got no *Zoqua* in me," he wheezed out, despite trying to sound defiantt. "I ain't got Zika virus or HIV or nothing. I clean." He tried to pull her hand away, but it barely moved.

"You not lying," she said, releasing him. "But something mark you for Zadoq'ua."

"What's this ... *Zathoqua*?"

"A creature. A god with the power to destroy everything."

"That why you attack me before? Because you think I work fo' he?"

"My head not been working right that day. I had poison in me from a fight before, so when I see evil in you, I couldn't hold back."

He looked her over. She seemed ashamed of her actions, and seeing how calm she was even while threatening him, he could understand why. Lashing out was not her natural inclination.

Danesh asked, "You the one kill the whale?"

She nodded her head regretfully. "In the end, yes. Was fo' mercy. But I was protecting it at first. From the dagonites. Is them who–"

The other fairmaids turned and began disappearing through the walls. The last one tapped Silverhair on the shoulder signalling impatiently that they should go. The girl stuffed the gag back into place and Danesh screamed through it as she backed away. Her big soft eyes blinked, seemingly in recognition of his plight. "I can't allow you to make noise, but..."

She waited until the last soldier had left, then pushed him down and roughly flipped him onto his chest. The sponge-rope on his wrists unwrapped itself and Silverhair turned and placed the rope in one of the pouches strapped to her thigh. She moved her finger along the wall, tracing a pattern it seemed and then walked through. So that was how you opened the locked door.

Danesh stood and walked over to where the 'door' was, shaking out his sore arms. He had noticed that the gel only opened when the user tapped the wall first. He tried his own palm, tracing designs and slapping it in different rhythms. The sound of the thumps reverberating around the room was drum-like and Danesh soon lost himself in playing the wall, 'donk-donk-doddonk,' using the fingertips and the heel of his hand just like with a dolak at the temple.

He was in the prison cell for hours he was sure, bored enough to experiment with the way the drum tones changed from the centre of the walls to the corners and from the tops to the bottoms.

But eventually, he was defeated by the wait and ended up prone on the floor, tapping a familiar beat half-heartedly on it while he mumbled through his gag, "Ah ha ayee milan ki bela..." He took a sighing breath through the chalky rope. "...deko ayee..."

Silverhair walked through the wall. She was holding a bowl and a cup, both made of stone.

Danesh had thought that when someone finally removed his gag, the first thing he would do was try to talk his way out of his trouble. He wasn't as good at sweet talk as *Aja*, but he knew the principles. On seeing the food, however, he realized he would probably need to keep his complaints until after he had eaten. Yet, when Silverhair actually removed his gag, he found he had more practical concerns rising up to his attention. "Hey, I got fo' go pee bad. You can't lock a man up like this and don't give he no toilet!"

"So just go in the corner." She pointed dismissively.

"What? No! I ain't some animal. I need proper facilities. I don't know how long you gon' keep me here, so I ain't smelling up the floor I got fo' sleep pon."

"The floor got more sense than you," said Silverhair, tapping a pattern with her foot. The gel flowed upward in defiance of gravity and solidified into the shape of a table and two stools.

"Oh," Danesh said as she put the food down. He looked over to the corner and then back at the girl. "Well, you still got fo' go outside and wait til I done."

"I can see everything you do in this room from outside."

"I don't care. A man can't just do he business when people right there."

She made an exasperated sound and left after again tracing the 'security code' pattern in the door. He walked over to the corner and reached out a toe to tap the ground. No reaction. He had been expecting a big toilet bowl to grow out of the ground. Oh, well. If this didn't work, he would make her change his cell. Somehow.

He lowered his briefs by the elastic waistband and started to relieve his bladder. As the stream landed on the floor, it soaked right into it, and Danesh realized the gel was channeling the liquid away somehow. Magic probably, he thought as he continued. Halfway through, he realized that Silverhair probably wasn't the only one able to see into this jail cell. There could be a whole ring of people watching him. He hurriedly finished and turned back to the table.

Silverhair came back in and said, "You not gon' clean you hands?"

"You don't got no water."

"Just wipe it on the wall. The *mojh* gon' take care of it."

Skeptically, Danesh wiped one hand on the gel surface of the wall. It felt momentarily wet and made a slurping sound, then returned to normal. He cleaned the other hand then came over and sat before the food.

The bowl was full of large shrimp, peeled and steamed it appeared, with flecks of purple and white seasoning on the surface. Danesh had half expected some kind of horrible, slimy mush for his food, but now rebuked himself. Of course, it was just shrimp. What else would they eat here in the ocean?

Then he saw the cup. It was half filled with a milky white fluid in which long blades of seaweed were floating upright.

"What's this?"

"Nothing bad. Now eat. We got people waiting to talk to you."

"Good." He bit into a shrimp and it tasted normal, except for a tingling in the seasoning, like it had been cooked in rum. "I hope some of the people waiting is the police so I can–. Wait, y'all have police around here? Who I supposed to report to that I get kidnap? That *you* kidnap me?"

"We ain't got nothing here like what you call police, but is the proper authority holding you here."

Danesh took another piece of the tingly shrimp. He wasn't sure he trusted the drink in the cup, but his throat was getting dryer.

"No police?" he asked. "So what happen when people thief or murder?"

She looked at him like he had suggested an obscenity. "It does hardly ever happen. And they turn they self in and face justice."

"Suppose they run away?"

"Nobody don't run away."

"Suppose *I* run away."

"Then I gon' take another protector squad and come get you again."

Danesh tried a sip of the pseudo-milk, the stems of grass tickling his nose, their aroma reminding him of nutmeg and the fever grass his grandmother would sometimes boil for medicine. The flavour was fruity and sweet.

"Look," he said calming down, "I need some clothes. You think you could help me out with that?"

"Why? You cold?"

"No, but I feel kinda naked, you know?"

"So?"

"So I not like y'all. I like fo' cover up me skin."

"You want me to cover up me skin too?"

"I never say nothing about that."

"I know they got places up there where the men make the women cover up everything. I thought maybe–"

"No, I like your skin showing – I mean, I don't got no problem with you showing any part you want. Is you country, right? Do it you own way."

She scowled at his verbal slip. "Wait here. I coming back."

The seascraper levels were full of open spaces like town squares where people gathered standing in knots and sitting in circles and semi-circles. The ceilings here arched like a sky, the bright blue sea filtering down. It was midday now and through the outer walls, Danesh could see for miles in the clear water past the glittering tops of the other buildings.

Some of the people, Danesh could understand perfectly as he walked past the conversations and lectures that seemed to be going on, but most spoke in the squeaky voice his kidnappers had used.

"You gon' teach me how fo' open them doors?" Danesh asked as they walked through another gel wall. He was amazed at how the gel knew to let the silky fabric of his robe through, despite its almost non-existent weight.

Silverhair said, "So you can escape?"

He looked at their escort of four tall soldier women and made a 'you joking?' face.

A pair of small children ran up to stare at Danesh and chittered to each other. He glared at them and they giggled in fright and ran away.

He looked around the big hall they were in. "I notice y'all don't got a lot of children around here."

"We don't make a lot of children."

"How come I can understand when you talk?"

Silverhair tapped her earlobe where a tiny seashell earring hung. "This thing read you brain and make it possible to talk to anybody who near you. As long as one of we wearing a seashell, you can understand me in you language and I can understand you in me language."

"But it not giving me English. It giving me Creolese."

"Then you language is not English. Is Creolese."

"Oh."

Near the centre of the tower, there was a circular railing of coral with entryways in two places. Four people walked on to the flat stone platform within the railing. The *mojh* gel underneath extended like a giant cylinder and lifted them up through a circular hole in the ceiling and then retracted without the platform. Through the clear surface, Danesh saw that the *mojh* on the upper floor had smoothly taken the platform and sent it upward again.

It was an elevator.

When the platform came back down, his escorts prodded him onto it. Their platform dropped far too quickly for his stomach's comfort, past about twenty floors that seemed to be mostly social and recreational spaces. It put them off in a hall that was decorated with hanging sheets of gauzy material that gave it a soft look. Coloured stripes on the gel floor converged on one side where a semi-circular table sat on an elevated platform. The table was made of stone, not *mojh*. Rows of people in elaborate robes sat off to the sides on cushioned benches. There was no nakedness here.

A circular ring of gleaming metal took up most of the clear wall behind the table, focusing the view to create a backdrop of bright blue ocean. It was midday now and sunlight filtered through the water in vertical beams. A group of manta rays (*A flock? A herd?*) wound its way through the mottled sea.

In the hall, five figures sat behind the great stone table. They broke off their quiet conversation when Silverhair approached with Danesh.

An ancient looking woman with long, grey hair tied in a braid sat in the centre chair, which was made of a cushiony red material laid over a pearlescent frame. It seemed that whatever their hair colour started as, even fairmaids ended up grey. Her eyes were half-closed, as if she were struggling to hold the lids up and her lined face looked to her lap as her head drooped at the top of her thin neck. Even seated, she was leaning on a gnarled walking pole that was inlaid with glowing streams of *mojh*.

To her right sat a fairman with a pointed beard that curled out and up. Danesh wondered if that was natural or if he had to style it that way with *mojh*. To his right was the first light-skinned fairmaid Danesh had seen. She was baby-blue under her green robe. She seemed to be trying hard to hide a smile.

The other two council members looked typical of the city, one with red hair, the other with black, and kept their attention on the old lady.

The fairman stood, his back straight and stiff. His face seemed menacing, like it was in a permanent sour mood. "The prisoner ready for he trial?"

Silverhair snapped an earring into Danesh's ear and replied, "He ready."

The room buzzed now it seemed to Danesh. He leaned over to Silverhair. "Everybody can understand me now?"

"Yes."

He turned to the council and said, "This ain't fair. You can't just grabble people and put them on trial and they don't even got a lawyer."

No, shut you mouth. Don't get these people vex.

But the outrage had been building in him for too long. He pointed at Silverhair. "This girl attack me first. You can't blame me fo' fighting back. And nobody ain't even ask me for me side of the story. You just lock me up in a room without no door and–"

"Child," said the man. "You not on trial for any fight."

"No?"

"No." The man looked around the room. "We investigating how come you get mark by Zadoq'ua. You–"

Angry voices erupted at the back of the room and everyone

turned. A dozen red-skinned fairmaids strode in. Leading them was a broad-shouldered woman with silver hair in a tight braid. She carried a black-bladed *daki* and wore a crown that was styled to look like white fire.

"Princess Bejara," said the man on the council, "you can't just walk in here any time you like. We in the middle of important–"

"Don't talk to me," boomed out the new arrival. "I didn't swim thousands of miles fo' something that wasn't important. And I didn't do it fo' deal with no man neither. I come to the Apexa." She looked over at the old woman in the centre chair but the Apexa did not react.

The man somehow stiffened his spine even more. "Well, I talking for the Apexa. Til the day she say otherwise, I's she voice. We not like y'all, we got equality in Coral City. You gon' have to wait til we done here. This business concern Zadoq'ua."

"Is Zadoq'ua we come about too. He bringing war to everybody. We come to warn you and–"

"You want warn we?" the dark-haired fairmaid seated on the outside asked sarcastically. "Y'all practically worship them Old Ones and now–"

"We gon' listen to Bejara first," said the old woman – the Apexa – in a frail, but surprisingly clear, voice. Her chin rose minutely and she looked at Danesh. "Let the surface child wait. Put he fo' sit down. And keep he secure."

Danesh's main escort held his elbow firmly. "Come."

This was the first time he could understand her, now that he had his seashell translator, and her voice was deep and strong. She led him to an enclosure off to one side, where they could still see the council platform. The spectators in the chamber kept staring at him after the Apexa had addressed him, so he was grateful that the space, while open in the front, was sectioned off with shrouds of the gauzy woven material and provided privacy from the rest of the gallery.

"Who's them red-skin people?" he asked Silverhair.

"Abyssians. They left here a long time ago to live with different rules."

While they spoke, the Abyssian princess was arguing with the bearded man, whose name was Numah. Bejara was demanding a seat at the table so she could be part of the council.

"So, is a racial thing?" Danesh asked.

She looked at him, puzzled. "Why you think that?"

"They all red and most of you dark blue. I know this skin colour thing does get political sometimes."

"No, the Abyssians think that men should stay at home and look after the children and don't be in politics. But all the cities in Atlantis give men rights about a thousand years ago, so a set of the women went fo' start they own thing far away, far from the coast, out where they ain't got no Dreamtide portal. They make friends with the dagonites even, so they can survive down there."

"Ah," said Danesh, watching the confrontation on the council floor, "That's why she and Numah hate one another."

"The reason they all red," said Silverhair, "is that in the deep water that's the best way fo' hide and hunt."

"So you can control what colour you skin got?"

She shrugged. "Is not easy. It take a long time, like a surgery."

"What about the light blue lady then?"

"Stay away from she." Medusa pulled him close with a hard grip on his shoulder. "Seriously. She come from a place close to the land with shallow water. They like mess around with sailors and men from the land."

He smiled. "Oh, you mean they like fo' seduce we? You

sound like you jeal–"

"Sometimes fo' seduce them," she nodded. Then she went still. "Sometime fo' eat them. Sometimes one after the other."

He stared at her, but she showed no sign that she was joking.

Numah broke off his arguments with the Abyssians to give a rebuking stare at Danesh. He bowed his head feeling like he was back in school and some teacher was angry with him for talking in class. Best to freeze up.

But Silverhair leaned over and asked, "You got a name?"

"Danesh." He was still intimidated by Numah, so it took him a while after the meeting resumed to continue. "What's you name?"

"Medusa."

"You name after a monster?"

"Being a monster come from what you do, not what you look like. Even up on land where y'all tell the story wrong, she wasn't no monster. I proud to carry she name."

"But in the story, she get–"

The Apexa banged the bottom of her rod on the stone floor. The *mojh* strips in it flashed like lightning and the crack echoed to every corner of the hall.

The negotiations with the Abyssians had ended.

Numah stood. "By decision of the learned Apexa, Princess Bejara is given temporary acsension to the council as the representative of her people during this emergency. Her request for a change of Speaker is not granted. She and her people shall be shown to the royal guest quarters and given food and time to recover from their journey before the council resumes." Then the man looked at Danesh. "The fate of the surface child shall be decided then."

Danesh swallowed at the idea of these strange people

controlling what happened to him. Deciding if he ever got to go home again.

The room cleared slowly, audience members strolling about to chat or leaving the hall entirely. The five councillors disappeared at some point, but Danesh never saw where. He and Medusa remained sitting next to each other, their guards standing around them.

"You say this city is part of Atlantis," Danesh said to Medusa, "like from the real Atlantis that sink in the story? I thought that was just a legend."

"You in a city underwater with people who got tail like fish. You still don't believe the story true?"

Danesh thought about his situation. About how incredible it was to be in an actual city of fairmaids. He almost considered that he was dreaming it all up, but too many things were different from what he could ever have imagined.

"You know," he said to Medusa, "is funny how they call y'all fairmaid in them story back home, but you and the rest what I see all got dark skin."

"Yeah, y'all up there in the sunlight always thinking dark is bad so you twisting thing around. Like in them old stories about Medusa, she used to be dark, even before she get transform. But then surface people start tell the story different, say she used to be fair skin and then she behave bad and get turn dark-skin as punishment. And she get so vex about the change that she start kill people. Like just skin colour enough fo' murder people over?"

"Too bad she didn't had Fair and Lovely," said Danesh.

"What's that?"

"This soap from India. Girls does use it fo' lighten they skin. I know some of them in school would kill for fair skin."

"You serious?"

"Yeah. Why?"

Medusa's voice was full of cold contempt. "Because it stupid."

"Don't blame them. Is other people calling girls ugly for being dark, you think the girls shouldn't do something 'bout it?"

"They should find the people who call them ugly and knock they teeth out," Medusa said, with thoughtful savagery.

"Maybe that's what happen with Medusa – she attack people fo' calling she ugly, not because she hate she dark skin. And that's why they call she a monster."

The young fairmaid looked at him in surprise. He got the impression he had inadvertently rebutted her idea to beat up name-callers but couldn't quite see how.

She said, "You know about Medusa and Atlantis. You like them old story?"

Danesh shrugged. "I like hear about them, but I don't know a lot. Just one or–"

Medusa rose and pulled him up with her. "Come, we got time before things start up again."

"Time for what?"

Her eyes brightened. "Stories."

The elevator took them to another hall, one of those with groups of people listening in curved rows while one person stood on a dais and told stories.

Clearly storytelling was far more important here than back home.

"We shoulda stay in the council hall," said the head of the guards, a tall, wide-shouldered woman with a permanent frown.

"Oh, relax, Daphne, you know the council always delaying. We got a lot of time before we got fo' go back."

"What about me?" Danesh asked. "Is full daytime already, people back home gon' be looking for me."

"Don't worry about them," said Medusa, leading them to a group she seemed to recognise. "When you get back, it gon' still be the same night you left."

"How that?"

"Because you in the Dreamtide. Time run different here."

"Why? What make this place special?"

"That portal you come through to get here? Is not just a different place it bring you to. It kinda move you sideways like, so you a little outside you own world. Imagine you standing next to yourself. That's what this place like. Some people does call it the Eternal Ocean. You can travel through it fo' move quick from one place to another or you can stay and live in it like we."

Danesh made a face as he tried to figure out that description. The specifics of it defied his imagination, but he now understood why this city was so well hidden from the surface world.

The first story they sat in on was about Sun Wukong, the Handsome Monkey King who gets his name removed from the books of Death and fights Heaven just from his sense of indignation. The comical battles and the trickery which helped Sun Wukong batter and disperse the armies of Heaven had

Danesh chuckling all the way through.

"You like this?" Medusa asked him.

"Yeah. You don't? I wish I had a super-weapon like he cudgel. I would set some people straight. Like Miss Geeta."

Daphne grumbled, "The Monkey King story childish."

"Yeah, but it still funny. And he brave too. He know he gon' lose eventually but every time they come for him, he win. I don't think they gon' ever beat he."

"Oh, so you don't know the ending then?" Medusa asked.

The storyteller had only told one episode of the long saga. "How it end?" Danesh asked, worried. "What happen to he?"

"You can hear that another time. Let we go find a more mature story."

"Alright, old lady," Danesh teased her.

Medusa chose the myth of Sisyphus. It was similar in some ways to the Monkey King with Sisyphus finding ways to cheat Death. One time Death came for him with special handcuffs and Sisyphus started admiring them and asked Death to show him how they worked and then left Death trapped in his own chains. But unlike the Monkey King, Sisyphus wasn't always a good man. In fact, he was a murderer and a tyrant. So Danesh actually felt like justice had been served when the gods finally punished Sisyphus by making him spend eternity rolling a rock up a hill only to see it come rolling back down every time.

"That story kind of pointless," he told Medusa. "All that fighting and trickery he do and he didn't get nothing out of it. It make you wonder why he even bother in the first place."

"But you just say the Monkey King know he gon' lose in the end and you like when he fight."

"*Handsome* Monkey King. Call he by he full name."

But Danesh had no actual rebuttal for Medusa, though he kept trying to think of one. They drifted into another story.

The way the system worked, everyone took turns telling tales and at the end of one fairmaid's story, Daphne said, "The boy should tell us a story too."

The crowd heard her deep voice and everyone looked at Danesh, waiting. The spirit of the day's tales had him feeling adventurous and he hesitated only a little before allowing Medusa to nudge him onto the podium.

He looked out at the curious audience, including Medusa with her serious expression. He realized he had the perfect story: he told them of the time near the beginning of the world when Shiva and the other gods vied with the demons to churn the ocean for the secret to immortality. The ocean spewed up poison that overpowered them all with its heat and to save the world, Lord Shiva swallowed up all the poison. Except that even he became too hot and to keep himself from losing control, he had to 'cool down' using ganja.

Danesh finished his tale, expecting to see his audience scandalized by his mention of drugs. Instead, Medusa and the others thanked him with their applause as if had been just another tale. Even without generating any outrage, Danesh felt a sense of accomplishment in telling his story and telling it well. He couldn't remember the last time he had been proud of himself.

Then a new soldier approached and spoke to Daphne who then gripped Danesh's elbow. "Time for we to go back to the council."

"Hey! Is not iron I make out of." Danesh tried to twist away, but she was holding him too tight.

"Daphne," said Medusa, gently peeling the older woman's hand away, "Remember he not a criminal."

"Yeah, Daphne," Danesh mocked her while rubbing his freed elbow, "I ain't no criminal."

Medusa looked at him with a cold glare. "Not 'til the

Apexa say so at any rate."

"Things gone very bad," Princess Bejara said, beginning her addess to the council.

The Apexa still sat in the centre chair, looking ancient with her braided grey hair and Numah was still her right-hand man, but Bejara had been given the seat to her left and the others had shifted down.

Bejara was standing as she spoke to the crowd packing into the gallery. "We make friends with the dagonites since the time we move to the Abyss. Centuries now we trade and respect each other. Some of us even start worshiping Zadoq'ua out of habit."

From the way she looked down hesitantly at this point, Danesh suspected she had been one of those worshipers.

"But they just start attacking all of a sudden," Bejara continued. "Not even to take away nothing. Just blind killing. We had to stop all we farming and hunting and pull everybody back to the pyramid fortress in the centre of the city and my mother send me to warn you and get help fo' crush them."

She stared around the room defiantly, as if to say that her people needing help was no weakness. She gave a special look of contempt to Danesh where he was sitting, back in the private chamber to the side. "Zadoq'ua awake now. I know everybody think he down in he mud cave full of red light in the belly of the Earth, meditating, because the story say so, but we know different now."

She spoke with bitterness. "He don't care one way or the other for any worship or loyalty. He just want fo' rule. We know he been emperor of this world five times before and he only give it up each time because he had more interesting things fo' do. If he want fo' come again and take over, we can't stop he unless we unite. All of the cities, not just Coral City, but the whole Atlantis."

A sarcastic voice said, "And you want to be in charge of the war?" This was from Amara, the dark-haired fairmaid who had argued with Bejara earlier.

"We the ones that get attack. We the ones who know how fo' fight them. It make sense that we should lead and—"

"You not the only ones who get attack or who fight them," said Numah. "Every Atlantean city been to blows with the dagonites since we first fall into the sea. One of we own ranger just take on a squad of them after they attack a whale." He pointed at Medusa, who shifted in her seat.

"All that mean is that I right," said Bejara. "You know they coming for Coral City too."

The Apexa spoke. "We got a lot of concern for we sisters in the Abyss. We won't never turn we back pon them. We gon' help. But first, we must understand what really going on. We capture a boy from the land who got the mark of Zadoq'ua on he and—"

"I got a name, you know!" Danesh surprised himself by not just standing but addressing the entire council. This was against everything he had learned about authority in school. He should sit down, shut up and wait it out. But he had let his anger burst through earlier and now again he was challenging these elders. Even Numah, who had scared him earlier and the old lady with the loud stick. He took a step forward, into the full view of the crowd. "I's Haimchand Seeram, otherwise known as Danesh and you can't just–"

"Shut up!" said Bejara, her nostrils flared. She turned to Daphne. "Guard, tie he down if you got to."

Daphne leaned toward Danesh as if she were about to obey, then hesitated.

"Do it," said Bejara. "I don't want no–"

"Leave he alone!" said Numah.

Medusa stood close at Danesh's back, one arm linked protectively in his.

When a tense few seconds had passed, Amara said, "Come up here, Haimchand Seeram otherwise known as Danesh. Stand up in front of we and let we sort this out."

Danesh's burst of courage evaporated. Daphne was standing still just out of arm's reach giving no indication of what side she had settled on. Medusa made the decision for him, guiding him out into the main floor where she left him alone. He faced the stone table. "First of all, what you mean I have a mark? I don't even got a tattoo. My mother say she would kick me out the house if I ever get one."

"The mark ain't really something you can see," Amara said.

"Is more like a stench," Bejara joked contemptously.

Even though he knew the game she was playing, Danesh found himself nervously trying to sneak in a sniff of himself. Then he looked up at Amara, "Whatever happen to me, is not my fault. I never ask for it. Ever since I's li'l boy I got this thing where I can breathe and see under the water and I never ask for that so—"

"How young?" asked Bejara, suddenly serious.

"Six? Seven?"

The hall and the council chamber exploded in murmurs that fluttered around its walls until the Apexa banged her stick down.

"It clear now that this child—" she corrected herself. "That we guest, Danesh, ain't what we first suspect. We can't understand this situation without help. And now with the Abyssians under attack too, and Zadoq'ua looking like he loose in the world, we gon' have to convene the sponges."

Again, the room murmured. But Danesh was busy wondering if he heard right. "What you mean sponge?"

Once more, the old lady brought order with a whack on the stone floor. Danesh wondered how the surface hadn't cracked yet. Once things quieted down, the Apexa said, "Danesh right about one thing. He's a outsider and we can't just expect he to know everything about we. So I asking for a volunteer to counsel he and help represent he in—"

"Medusa," Danesh told them.

"What?" Numah asked.

"I should get fo' pick for me own self. So I pick Medusa."

"Medusa is a ranger. She got work outside the city fo' do and—"

"I ain't care. She's the only one treat me good this whole time and look at me like I's somebody."

"She try fo' kill you," Amara said.

"I rather that than the way the rest of you act like I don't got no rights and no say." Numah looked flustered, but before he could say anything, Danesh continued, taking advantage of the confident mood he was riding, "And if you got fo' wait for some stupid sponge thing, I ain't staying here. I going home and you can come get me when everything ready."

That last remark earned him a return to the prison cell.

He was there for an hour before Medusa showed up carrying food. It was fish this time with the same fruity milk drink.

"Why you provoke Numah?" she asked, raising the *mojh* table and stools from the floor and setting the food down. "The man like power. He not gon' take you disrespect like that."

Danesh gave her a sheepish look as he ate. All the bravado that had surged through him earlier had long died.

She shook her head in annoyance. "You like a li'l child sometimes, poking you hand in crab hole just because somebody tell you don't do it. You gon get clamp good and proper one of these days."

"I sorry. You right. I gon' be careful."

She pursed her lips sympathetically for just a moment. "Anyway," Medusa said, "I talk to the Apexa for you and she agree you can go home and wait."

"Really?" He looked around, expecting a prank.

"Yes. As long as you promise fo' come back. The Apexa say you look like you would keep a promise."

He took a few gulps of his fruity milk. Could these water people follow him if he ran away with *Aja* to some mountain top in the diamond bush? Or would that just be more childishness?

"Is what is this sponge thing I got fo' talk to?" he asked.

"Sponge is the oldest life on Earth. Some of them is ten or fifteen thousand years old. They wise. They know things. And they see things. Is like time don't work in a straight line for them. So when we got big problems we does ask them fo' help. We call them the Parliament."

"So how long 'til they ready?"

"Is like I tell you, time don't work the same with them. No way to know. That's why we only go to them for big things."

Danesh looked into her eyes. He saw more of that kind-hearted person he earlier had suspected her to be. She might act cold and scornful of others, but he was sure she understood pain and desire.

"Medusa," he said, "It would be okay if I come back before the oracle ready? Like just fo' hang out and hear stories and so?"

"Well, it gon' make my job more easy not having fo' watch you up there all the time. Sure."

He stepped onto the shore and went home to find that it was indeed the same night he had left, just as Medusa had promised. When he awoke, he had to keep working to convince his brain he had really been to Atlantis. Danesh was full of energy, as if he had enjoyed a full night's deep sleep. However long he had spent in the Dreamtide, he felt no effects. He ate breakfast with his mother – fried bakes with salted fish.

"That's new," he said, pointing to a circular black plaque a little larger than a dinner plate that had been hung in the living room. There was a white plastic ॐ in the centre with lots of little electric lights on concentric circles around it.

"It does light up," she said, walking over. "Look."

Blue, red, yellow and green lights flickered on and off, giving the effect of the light spiraling outward from the white light of the Om in the centre.

Danesh smiled, feeling a harmony in the movements. "I like it."

"Really?" She knew that *Aja* had been teaching him disrespect for religion, so he understood her surprise.

"Yeah," he reassured her. "It make the room look lively."

The stench of rotting whale was permeating the whole village by that second Monday morning. The government had sent two bulldozers and an excavator to the beach Danesh saw, but burying the massive carcass was proving beyond them.

Getting to school early for a change, Danesh went to his classroom, not in the mood for after-weekend catching up. What could he say to his friends? That he'd visited a secret dream city under the ocean after being kidnapped by a beautiful fairmaid? Oh, and that an evil god had put a curse on him?

He looked out the windows, most of them cracked or missing panes of glass. The ocean lay beyond the seawall looking dishwater grey and flat. How deceptive. He knew the truth about what was beneath the surface now.

He turned his attention back inside, to the unpainted concrete floor of the classroom, following the line of one crack into another with his eyes. This had always been a place where Danesh came to turn off his mind and his senses and wait out the school day until he could be himself again. Now he wanted to shout at it, to tear into it, beat it into submission. His hands curled into fists.

He started to look back towards the ocean, but sparkles of red, green, blue and yellow caught his eye. Parallel to the line of broken windows was a wet section of floor. Leftover beads of rain on the tops of the desks were scattering the morning light, transforming themselves into rainbow jewels. The colours drew Danesh into a relaxed trance and his breathing slowed. A deep 'mmmmmhm' sound rose from his chest – the rumbling sensation calming his brain. His hands relaxed.

But his peace only lasted moments as the school bell clanged discordantly. Outside in the pseudo-courtyard, he saw the school secretary at the office door, labouring with both arms to swing the brass hand bell.

The school lined up by class for assembly, so Danesh was soon with Robot and the others in Grade 9C while they stood to attention and said the National Pledge. Nadira was in 9B, so she stood directly in front of them in her own line. From time to time, she would turn and make subtle insult faces at Robot.

The morning heat was rising and Danesh found himself ignoring the others as he zoned everything out, anticipating the boredom of another assembly.

But this was no ordinary day. As Miss Corrine finished her usual tally of announcements and admonishments, she shifted her voice, becoming officious. "Children, our country is in a terrible crisis. As some of you may have heard recent figures show that we in Guyana have the highest suicide rate in the world. And Essequibo has the highest rate in Guyana. And most of the people taking their own lives are young people like you." Her accusing tone of voice at the end was meant to make Danesh feel guilt that his generation had brought shame to his country. That might have worked last week. Today he had enough internal defiance to think that Miss Corrine was wrong about him. Danesh thought of the Handsome Monkey King and smiled to himself.

Then he caught Miss Geeta staring at him and he quickly slipped on his well-practiced blankness.

On stage, Miss Corrine said, "Now, listen carefully," and swept her eyes over the students. "We will be having a visitor this afternoon from the Ministry of Health – a doctor! – to give you a very important talk about suicide. I'm warning you right now that you are all to sit quietly and pay proper attention. Anyone who makes this school look bad will be severely punished."

The suicide talk was in the afternoon. During the day, Danesh had time to eat his lunch with Robot and Nadira. The big news was that Susie, she of the fair-skinned legs, was now living in Georgetown.

"Amit gon' go crazy," Robot said, the pick in his hair moving with his shaking head.

"He want fo' go live in town too," Danesh said skeptically.

"And do what? He can't get no proper job."

Nadira sucked her teeth with disgust. "I don't know why he obsess with that girl. She full of she'self."

"You sound jealous," Robot said.

Danesh left their erupting argument behind. As much as he had always enjoyed their banter, he was feeling a separation between himself and everyone else. Like he was an alien visiting the planet.

Four clangs of the bell rang out during classes that afternoon. Danesh hated the harsh sound, but it had at least saved him from Sir Karan's English class. The young teacher had been making fun of Danesh's inability to read a comprehension passage. This time he didn't have to hear the usual ending to such episodes, where Sir Karan would say to the class, "Why you students don't care about you future? None of you don't want to put in any effort. You just expect to learn by sitting there like mud."

But escaping Karan only put him in Miss Geeta's path. She stopped him and his whole class as they filed into the assembly area. Her big blunt finger pointed at his chest. "You been laughing this morning when Miss Corrine was trying to explain something very important."

"No, Miss, that wasn't–"

"Don't back talk me, boy! I see you. You had better remember what she told the school this morning. Keep you damn mouth shut."

He joined Robot and Kevitt on a bench designed for two. This was a double classroom, with a stage and lectern at one end. For presentations and shows, they removed the desks and brought in extra benches from the room next door. By fitting the children three to a bench, they made the whole school fit inside the space. Miss Geeta's delay meant no window seat, however, so he was already sweating in the poor ventilation.

The speaker, Dr. Franklin, was about thirty, a woman with an eager expression and her hair in a neat ponytail that made her seem friendly despite her dark green pantsuit.

After she was introduced by Miss Geeta, Dr. Franklin said in an upbeat voice, "Good afternoon, everyone. I'm so glad to have this chance to speak with you. I was at the school down the road this morning and we had a wonderful session. They were full of questions and stories and it was quite productive."

The school down the road, of course, was the one his cousin went to, the one for all the bright students. The ones who could read well. Who never got mixed up in maths. And who studied even when they didn't have to.

The doctor looked around the room, waiting for some sign of welcome, but everyone stayed quiet.

"Right," she said, "So, um, to start out, I need to ask a very important question: how many of you know someone who has attempted or committed suicide?

Students kept their gazes blank as they sweated in the hot room. No one dared be the first to draw attention. Two rows away, Danesh saw Anna, whose big brother had drunk poison last year after he failed his CSEC exams. Near the front of the room, right under the doctor was Ravin. His twenty-year-old sister had hung herself after her religious parents had decided she couldn't marry her boyfriend. Sitting near the window was Dookie. His uncle had taken poison when he ran his welding business into more debt than he could pay. In the back corner of the room, Danesh saw an older boy named Mahesh who had his head down as he blinked wetness from his eyes. Mahesh had tried to kill himself a year ago, but his parents had gotten him to the hospital in time to have his stomach pumped.

Up on stage, the silence was taking a toll on the doctor's enthusiasm. Danesh could read her face more easily than if he had Clearsight into her brain. No doubt she had been told before she arrived that this was the 'dunce' school and had not believed it. Outsiders often came with the attitude that any kid could be taught. But she was starting to believe that these students were indeed never going to contribute anything. Either to her event or even to the world.

Accepting defeat, Dr. Frankin delivered her presentation without asking for any more participation while the students kept silent under the gaze of their supervising teachers.

When she had done telling them about depression, warning signs, and the awful statistics, Dr. Franklin ended by giving them the number for the Ministry's mental health hotline. "I know a lot of people say that no one answers the phone when they call, but we don't have any psychiatrists in this part of the country." She shrugged. "So, the helpline is all I have to offer you."

With shoulders slumped, the doctor accepted the principal's thanks and left, no doubt headed back to her air-conditioned office in Georgetown.

After their workout that night, Jones and Danesh went next door to the library. As he sat in front of the computer, listening to Jones talk about different ways to access a database, Danesh understood what it meant to be 'pumped up'. The workout had been tough, but with everything that had happened in Coral City, he felt more than ever that there was a need for him to be strong and prepared.

Not just physically either. His computer skills, which had been a tool to access forbidden images now seemed like a means to become more.

More what, he wasn't quite sure yet. He looked at the shelves of books around them. A fourth-grader sat in the corner reading a Spiderman comic Danesh knew was beyond his own skill. He hoped Jones didn't try to force him to read a computer book as part of his training.

Danesh seemed to be learning well enough without it anyway. He interrupted Jones. "So that command you just used, could I use it to connect a different way, like this?" He tapped the keyboard to show what he meant.

"Meh. It might work, but it wouldn't be efficient." Jones squinted at Danesh. "How come you can read and write good when you at the computer? The dyslexia don't affect you?"

Danesh shrugged. "Just too busy thinking about the structure and the way the information moving. I just kind of forget fo' be dyslexic."

"Yeah, dyslexia can be that way. You just got to figure out a way to focus around it like." Jones began setting up a new scenario on the screen. "Danesh, they don't got nobody at you school that deal with that kinda thing? A reading teacher?"

"They put me in remedial reading me first year, but the teacher just didn't had time for everybody. She try li'l bit, but the next year they put me back in the regular class."

Jones rubbed his lower lip with a thumb. His voice was strained when he spoke. "Is a very unfair system they got, the way they split up kids into good schools and bad schools just from how they do on a exam at a young age. People like you need extra care."

"But everybody say the system more fair this way because children who deserve it get the attention and they can help develop the country."

A sad look came over Jones' face. "But the system not fair,

Danesh. You ever look at the big attendance board in the office at you school?"

"No." The old Danesh had never been curious about things like that.

"Well your school got a hundred more boys than girls. And the school right down the road for the bright children got a hundred extra girls. You think girls better than boys somehow?"

"Well, no. I mean some girls and some boys, but–"

"But if it was a fair system, it would be even, right?"

"Right. Like in statistics when–"

"And your school got more poor kids too," said Jones. "You ever notice that?"

"Not really."

"I can't say why it work out so unbalanced, but I know it can't be because the system fair."

A woman in an office dress looked in at the main door and called away the girl reading the Spiderman book. Danesh looked around to make sure he and Jones were the only ones left.

"Mr. Jones, you ever hear about something name Zadoq'ua?"

"Nope. Sounds old."

"Yeah, he suppose to be real old. But I never hear about he in no legend or in history."

"Well, they got an easy way to find out. Just–"

"Please don't say a book."

"Internet. Spell this name for me?" Jones went 'hmm' and 'aha' for a few minutes and then said, "This look like the place. Reddit."

"Zadoq'ua don't got nothing to do with love, trust me."

"Lovecraft was a writer. Most people think he was writing stories but some people say he and some other writers was putting down history that they was seeing in they dreams." Jones clicked around some postings on the screen then said mockingly, "I think this website full of people who worship these old gods or something."

"And one of them writers put down stuff in a book about Zadoq'ua?"

A painting popped onto screen. It showed a gigantic creature, squatting in the shadows of a muddy cave on clawed feet. It had a round pot-belly and spindly arms with long three-fingered claws of their own. The monster's head was wide, with bulging eyes and pointed ears topped with wild tufts of long hair. And inside the creature's wide mouth was a wide tongue dripping slobber between a hundred small teeth.

A shock of recognition went through Danesh and he backed away from the screen, toppling his chair. But it coudn't be recognition. He'd never seen this thing before. Why did he feel like he knew it?

"You scared of a picture?" Jones asked, amused.

"I ... I wasn't expecting nothing like that is all. Ugly."

"Yeah." Jones pulled up a few more paintings, each an imagining of roughly the same creature. "Anyway," he said, "enough of that. Let we get back to work."

But Danesh couldn't concentrate. Now that he had finally seen the creature that was going to take over the world – and who had marked him somehow – his brain could not rest.

"Monsters not real you know," Jones told him as he shut down the computer in frustration at Danesh's lack of focus. "Not that kind anyway."

"Wait," said Danesh, suddenly paying attention. "What kind real?"

"People. They got people in this world do monstrous things all the time. *That* scare me."

"Yeah, I know what you mean."

84

Jones looked at him directly. "Somebody hurting you, Danesh?"

"No, I don't mean that. I just know–" He took a breath. "When I been about eight or nine, me grandfather used to get me fo' help he thief bicycle."

"That's a crime, but it's not anything monstrous."

"No, listen. I need to explain first. The way it work, my grandfather would pick a bike outside the big supermarket and he would tell me which one and then walk away. And I would go pick up the bike like I own it and just wheel it down the road. And then Aja would give me some pocket change and I would go back to the supermarket to buy ice-cream. The two of we used to treat it as one big joke."

Danesh shook his head as he remembered. "One day, I licking away at me cone and this man come up and say, 'Hey, li'l boy, come help me find me bike.' He wasn't old, but he look old, and I could smell rum pon he breath. Thing is, I know I was the one take away he bike right before, so I trying to act innocent and I agree fo' help he search. We check the whole area around the parking lot and there ain't got no bike fo' find.

"So, the drunk man, he say, 'Is alright, son, I glad you try and help.' And then he put he hand pon me hair and rub it and add, 'You look like me son, you know that? He was a helpful boy too. Always looking out fo' people. He always use to tell me he would be a doctor when he grow up.' And then the drunk man get sad and he say, 'But they kill he. Just ten year he been and somebody take he and cut he throat side to side.'

"And then he start fo' walk away, but he turn back and slap me across me face and holler at me, 'Why you out here alone? You don't know they got bad people around here? Li'l boy like you shouldn't be out late night like this.'

"The security guard come and chase he away after that.

85

Then the guard tell me I mustn't hold it against the man because he was a good man before and is only since he son dead that he does drink too much and behave crazy."

Danesh looked at Jones. "I stop thiefing bicycle after that. I tell me *Aja* it wasn't no fun no more and he say okay."

After a slight hesitation Danesh decided there wasn't any point to telling Jones that the drunk's son had been murdered by his uncle, so instead he just said, "So yeah, you right. Whoever kill that boy, they's like a real monster. In they brain at least."

The next week was one of wonder and thrills. Each night, Danesh would open the portal with his pendant and swim through to Coral City. He would spend hours listening to legends at the speaking halls with Medusa or she would take him out into the wild ocean to see things only a ranger would know about.

He always asked if there was word from the Parliament of Sponges or if the war with the dagonites was starting, but she always shrugged and told him that things would take as long as they needed to take. Then he would soon bury his worries about Zadoq'ua for a few hours while he listened to the tales.

The best stories were the ones where heroes took on monsters and quests to restore justice to the world using their wits and courage. Danesh especially liked if the end was terribly bloody, like the Seven Sisters' Trials where they had their teeth knocked out or Theseus battling the half-bull Minotaur. Theseus reminded him of his grandfather in the way he seduced the king's daughter into betraying her father and finding him a path out of the Labyrinth maze with a golden thread.

Danesh had considered telling his grandfather about Coral City and the Dreamtide in the first few days after he was snatched away by Daphne and her protector squad. But he knew his grandfather wouldn't believe him. The old man was very dismissive of anything to do with religion or spirits or magic. So the Dreamtide became Danesh's private playground.

From the start, he tried to be a better storyteller. He didn't treat his second time speaking in the hall as a joke, but told a serious story, about the wreck of a ship named Medusa two hundred years before. He took his time giving his audience the gruesome details of how 140 people had tried to escape to safety on a raft the size of a large carpet while being pulled by a boat. Of how the boat had abandoned them with just a box of biscuits. Of how they had died gradually, either killed by the sea, killed by each other or choosing to kill themselves, until only fifteen men had survived, living on the flesh of their friends. But the best part for Danesh was at the end when he revealed to his listeners that it had been a *true* story.

As they were leaving to find dinner, he told Medusa, "Was a true story for real you know. I find it on the internet when I did looking up more about Medusa." He looked back at the crowd. "They ain't look too impressed, though."

"Boy," said Medusa, "you still thinking that them old story is fairy tale. But real and make believe don't got no meaning around here. All is just 'story' to we."

They continued talking even when Medusa led him into the ocean because they could communicate mind-to-mind under the water when they each wore an earring. She opened a portal for them.

"Where you taking me?" Danesh asked silently.

"Fo' see the real ocean."

The real ocean according to Medusa began in a kelp forest. The water was nearly a hundred feet deep. Long streamers of yellow-green leaves stretched up to the rippling sunlight above. The roots of these underwater stalks were anchored in the rocky bottom. There was enough separation to allow Danesh and Medusa to swim between the shadowed spaces in comfort, brushing the leaves with their hands. They met a small, whisker-faced seal near the top of the forest. It ran off at first but soon returned to follow them. Medusa held out her hand and eventually got the hesitant animal to bump its nose against her palm. Danesh tried, but the animal seemed to detect something disgusting as it sniffed his fingers and darted away.

"Why he do that?" he asked. "You think maybe he smell Zadoq'ua on me like Bejara say?"

"No. The mark don't work like that. It take–" Medusa froze, even her tail hanging motionless. "Danesh," she said, looking slowly around, "Stay quiet and sink down with me."

"Why? What happ–"

"Just do it!" she shouted in his head.

He obeyed, heading for the murky bottom and crouching there with her.

From out of the hazy, distance a great white shark glided into view. Danesh's insides went watery at the sight of the huge triangular teeth, each one as long as his finger. The shark was gracefully sliding by the kelp stalks, its large, dead-looking eyes held still.

He reached for Medusa's hand and held it firmly. He didn't care how cowardly that made him seem.

Eventually, the great beast swam off into the hazy distance and Danesh turned to Medusa. "You bring me to get hunt by shark? What wrong with you?"

"Relax, as long as you stay out of they way, they don't bother you."

"I don't care. Take me home."

"Fine, the portal over this way. We can go back to Coral City and—"

"No, no. Not Coral City. I going back home to Guyana. I done with ocean. I ain't looking fo' get eat."

But he was back the very next day, listening to more tales under the waves.

During a break, Medusa took him to eat in her quarters. "You got parents?" he asked her as they walked into the chambers. Like most Coral City apartments, it had an open floor and walls without detail – until the right code was tapped on a waiting surface. Set next to the window was a rectangular tank filled with water, the edge as high as Danesh's waist, and the top open. Was that for bathing? Did ocean people need to bathe?

"Me parents don't live in Coral City," Medusa said as she brought up a *mojh* couch and a table from the floor. Danesh sat on the couch, finding it soft and deep, almost like being swallowed by water.

The wall where the 'door' had been buzzed and glowed. Medusa opened it and let Daphne in.

Danesh scowled. "What you doing here? Me and you ain't got no more business."

Daphne scowled back. "I wish I left you alone, but the Apexa say I got fo' protect you."

"He gon' be okay," said Medusa. "I's a ranger. I can handle any animal come after he in the water."

"Is not animal the Apexa worrying about," said Daphne, walking in, her *daki* held firmly in one hand. "Some people think is a mistake fo' let the boy live. They want assassinate he rather than tolerate Zadoq'ua magic in the city."

"Who people?" asked Danesh, standing and looking about.

"People," said Daphne, shrugging then standing silently.

Danesh sat back down but found it impossible to eat with Daphne watching him. Medusa walked through an archway into an adjacent room.

"You really a ranger?" he asked her, trying to get comfortable. "You kinda young for a big job like that."

"I ... I in training you could say. We don't got high school, so we just pick a job early and start doing it."

"Me friend Amit like that. He leave school and say it ain't no use to he. Now he working and learning while he work."

Danesh got back up and stood near the pool of water. A few red and yellow fish chased each other outside the window. He could see Medusa in the other room, raising a table from the ground.

"So where you parents live exactly?" he asked.

"Somewhere else," Medusa said with sarcasm.

He leaned back against the lip of the pool, resting his hands on the solid edge as he watched her fiddle with a cylinder-shaped apparatus. He said, "That's what you make food with? It don't smell li– Aaaahhgh!"

A tentacle had emerged from the pool and coiled around his wrist. He pulled away, but two more of the red and white tentacles emerged and grabbed his forearm, holding with powerful muscles. As he staggered back, he saw that an octopus the size of a large dog was entering the pool from the ocean side and his motion brought it through the *mojh* wall, out of the pool, and into the dry room. Danesh continued to scream as he fell on his back, the swarming tentacles grabbing both his arms and restraining them.

Medusa came out of the room and shouted, "Don't move! Don't hurt he." She ran over and gently lifted the octopus onto her shoulder, stroking its over-sized head as it wrapped itself all around her. The wide webbing between the tentacles made it seem like she was wearing a kind of cloak.

Danesh got to his feet, wiping the slimy wetness off his forearms. "Is the octopus you was talking to?"

"Alpata got a lot of sense. *She* can understand plenty."

He looked over at Daphne, who had not moved or spoken throughout the 'attack'. "I thought you here to protect me?"

"Is just a octopus. Stop acting like a li'l child."

Danesh shook his head in annoyance. He wanted to clean his arms in the pool water, but who knew what would come through that wall next? He wiped them off on the *mojh* walls instead while Medusa put the octopus into its tank. It floated with half its massive head above the water, watching Danesh, while its tentacles waved slowly under it.

"That thing just come and go whenever it want?" he asked.

"Yeah. I teach she the code to open the *mojh* from outside the tank."

He checked his arms for cuts. There were none. Just some bruising. "What it does eat?"

"Whatever she want. She does go outside when she hungry. I gon' show you."

After they ate a lunch of raw fish and a kind of vegetable

noodle, Medusa led Alpata and Danesh to a stretch of coral outside the city, Danesh keeping his distance from the octopus. Daphne hovered nearby.

The reef proved to be a kingdom of colour and motion. Fishes would scamper past singly and in multitudes, changing direction at random, flashing in the light. The floor was littered in treasure: curly starfish, spiky anemones, twisted sponges, blossom-like sea slugs, spiral seashells, comical crabs and elegant coral formations. A grey-green patch of ground began to undulate and turned into a moray eel, its wide sharp-toothed jaws making it look like a grinning idiot.

Alpata jetted a cloud of dark red ink at the eel and hid behind Medusa.

"Them eel like eat octopus," she explained and the four of them swam off.

On the way back, they found Bejara's soldiers training. Medusa stiffened into a look of focused hate as she watched, stunning Danesh with how quickly she had transformed from his helpful guide to the warrior who had attacked him that first day on his boat. With a little bit of trepidation, he reached out and nudged her elbow. "Come, let we go home."

Medusa's gills flared as she took a deep breath and then continued swimming.

The Abyssians were using coral formations to practice ambushes with their black-bladed *dakis*. As they moved with speed and grace and savagery, Danesh was again struck by Bejara's distinctive silver hair. She gave the two of them a look of contempt as they swam by.

"She really don't like y'all," said Danesh.

"We and them don't value the same same things," said a voice from above.

It was the Apexa. She swam gracefully down to the coral

reef from the sparkling surface, her pale hair flowing ethereally behind her and her tail effortlessly brushing the ocean aside. Danesh couldn't believe this was the same old lady slumped in the council chair earlier.

Even her face seemed younger with her eyes wide open and the lines of her face smoothed out away from the dryness of the air. Whereas she had carried her stick like a crutch in the chamber, now she wielded it like a weapon.

Danesh forced himself to be silent, afraid of blurting something impolite about how she didn't look ugly in the water.

The Apexa stopped next to him and her regal voice filled his head. "Bejara and she people, they always want action first instead of thinking about problems."

"Yeah, but I think they got the right idea. They look ready fo' fight Zadoq'ua and the dagon people and whoever else get in they way. I ain't see none of you people out here. Y'all even got a real army?"

"Everybody gon' fight when the time come, son." She smiled at him. "It okay if I call you 'son'?"

He didn't like it, but he was grateful she was asking first, so he nodded.

"War does take preparation," she said. "We got fo' organise food and weapon and shelter and all that first. Come, let me show you." She flicked her tail at him and send a bubbly rush of water at his face as she swam away.

The octopus went off on her own and the Apexa led Danesh and the others to a low building near the shallow side of the city. Inside were rows and rows of stone tables, scooped out into shapes like slim trays with metal rods inserted lengthwise. Over at one end of the building, workers were placing small seashells into the trays and filling them with slime-green water before covering them with a sheet of *mojh*. "Seashell is one of the hardest substance in the world. We got a way to make the shell grow in the shape we want, so it turn into a *daki* blade around the metal."

She walked to the end of the 'factory' floor where she held up a finished blade by its ensconced rod. The surface shone like polished ivory and the light seemed to spark on the sharp edges.

Danesh asked, "How long to grow one though?"

"A week, maybe two."

"And suppose you get attack tomorrow?"

She flicked her nail against the blade, making a pinging sound. "Then, my son, we gon' fight with what we got and if we lose, we lose. But it–"

"You mean 'if you dead, you dead'."

"It don't make sense fo' rush and don't prepare properly. You mightn't see it, but deep down, the people in this city getting ready for war."

A few days later, Danesh was eating with Medusa when the walls of her tower began to shake. By now, Alpata trusted Danesh enough to let him pet her and he no longer thought of her as dangerous and ugly. The octopus sensed the quake first and gave a warning squeal before it climbed off the dry floor and up into its tank before exiting. Once Medusa and Danesh were outside between the buildings, the site that greeted him was almost as comical as it was scary. The buildings were shaking like jello as the earth moved under them, but their bending easily kept them from breaking. After the quake, Medusa casually returned to eat.

"It don't make you nervous?" Danesh asked.

"Nah. We does get li'l tremor all the time around here."

As the days of exploring the many strange worlds of the ocean continued, they found themselves ending the visits by sitting on the beach at Tiger Island. It was his idea and he explained that he had always felt a kinship with this stretch of wilderness.

This was the eastern beach, a thin strip of brown sand which they always had for themselves. No one lived on the island anymore. Farmers came over by boat to plant rice and a watchman sometimes stayed over on the inland side to watch the tractors and the diesel tanks. Their isolation led to a greater sense of intimacy and they talked more freely.

He told her about his family and friends and about school. She told him about her journeys in the ocean and her struggles to become a full-fledged ranger. That was how he found out that she had never had a boyfriend.

"Really?" he asked. "Never?"

"Man and woman don't pair in we society. There ain't enough men. So the women, they does take turn with the men and the men all live together and raise the children."

"Not Numah."

"He different. He got ambition fo' change how things work."

"So all the woman don't get lonely?"

She shrugged. "We got one another."

"You mean like...?" Well, that made sense. And now that he thought about it, he had seen quite a few all-female pairs in the city.

"So, you too?" he asked Medusa.

"Sometimes."

"You don't feel like you want a man?"

She looked him up and down, then smiled. "Eventually. Is not time yet."

It was during one of these pre-sunrise talks that a feeling like an invading swarm of bees began throbbing in Danesh's skull. He held his temples and groaned.

"Stop joking around," Medusa said, "I done tell you, raw fish won't make you sick."

"Something calling," he gasped out. "Something want me fo' go–" His mind cleared suddenly. The pain and its accompanying dread seemed to have never been, replaced by sense of being pulled. Danesh stood and walked towards the tall mangroves at the top of the beach.

"Danesh?" Medusa called.

But he ignored her, too intent on the sense of urgent need. She grabbed his shoulder and looked ready to shout at him. He put a finger up. "Something from over there. I feel it in me head." He pointed through the trees across the dark, flooded tops of the newly planted rice fields.

In the dim moonlight a dark stone steeple stood up amongst a grove of silk-cotton trees. On either side were ruined buildings. "This was where all the people used to live long ago. They leave because of flooding before me grandfather did born."

"But nobody here now?"

"Not supposed to be."

They walked through the slippery mud of the paths, their bare feet sometimes sinking ankle deep. June was near the end of the rainy season and the dirt roads on the flat island had become like swamps, complete with mosquitoes that bit him with every step.

Danesh fought to ignore it as he kept his eyes focused on the church near the centre of the island. Near the bridge that led to the churchyard was a sign that Danesh had never bothered reading on his previous visits: St. Peter's Church, constructed 1855. Over to the right were the remains of the old estate house, a wide, two-story building that had once sported an enclosed veranda that had now fallen in on itself, leaving planks of hanging wood. To the left were the stone remains of an old rice mill, the curves of the old cast-iron wheels silhouetted against the uneven brick walls standing amid the wild shrubbery.

But the church yard itself was like a cave, covered by the high, broad branches of the silk-cottons. Danesh swatted at a mosquito that pierced his neck with what felt like a hot needle.

He noticed Medusa, who was quietly watching the treetops and asked, "Them mosquito not bothering you?"

"The *mojh* pon me skin keeping them away. Is like armour."

He stepped on the planks of the bridge, avoiding the places where a few had gone missing. A terrible churning sound started under his feet. "Don't stop," said Medusa with a hand in his back. Once they were on solid ground he leaned down and looked under the bridge. The shallow water in the drainage ditch was packed with toads, each the size of his head. They had stopped their leaping and now their eyes stared at him, unblinking.

He backed away and turned to the tall, steep roof of the church which stood out against the stars. A circular bell-tower stood above the church to one side, maybe six stories tall to the top of the metal cross mounted on its pointed tip. They walked up to the wide arch of the entrance, but the door was locked.

They circled to the side to look into the windows, but the inside of the building was too dark to make out anything, even with most of the glass panes broken. At the back, the churchyard was overgrown with bushes that rose up in the spaces between the raised tombs. They came back around to the side with the bell tower. The base of the tower was easier to see into through the metal gate that gave entry. It creaked open at Danesh's push and the grating of the metal against the stone floor sent an echo of the earlier pain into his mind. He leaned his head into the entrance and looked up. The wooden stairs circling up into the top of the tower had broken clean off from the sides in at least two places. The dark, circular shape of a massive bell hung above, unreachable for them.

He stepped inside and his foot slid on the wet floor. He looked down, letting his eyes adjust to the light and his Clearsight kicked in, revealing every detail – enhancing them in fact.

There was blood covering the floor, streaked where his

foot had lost its grip. The pool of red had come from the corpse of a baby goat, its guts freshly spilled onto the stone from a single slit in its belly.

Danesh backed out of the doorway, knocking Medusa back in his haste. "Oh God." He knelt in the thick grass and vomited.

"What in there?" Medusa asked as she helped him up.

"Somebody kill a animal," he told her. "What I feel must be when it die. We got fo' go in case the people who do this still around."

That was their last visit to the beach.

Medusa was helping him improve his navigation the day the summons came. They had been working on it for weeks because his dyslexia seemed to also affect his sense of direction. With her help he had learned to identify his triggers and missteps and most importantly to persist with his efforts.

Daphne wasn't there as they moved through the reef, having been called away, but she soon returned with a cohort of serious-faced soldiers. "The council get notice that the Parliament ready for Danesh. We leaving immediately." She reached for his wrist then stopped and opened her hand in an inviting gesture. "Come."

"What?" he asked. "I don't get a chance fo' dress good or get ready?" He was wearing only jeans, as he usually did on his visits.

"Them sponge won't care if you go naked," said Medusa swimming past him.

The delegation to the Sponges was impressive: twenty soldiers, all five councillors, Bejara, three priestesses, three engineers, three generals, and a dozen ambassadors from other cities who had arrived since the news of Zadoq'ua's awakening. Everyone wore flowing ceremonial robes.

"I thought them sponge don't care about clothes," Danesh said to Medusa.

She smiled. "Yes, but I didn't say other people don't care."

They swam up from the city towards the surface and a portal appeared. It had a red flare around it instead of the usual blue.

Danesh still heard the familiar and comforting *ummmb* sound as they went through, so that eased his nerves. On the other side they found a black mountain, its sides so flat that it didn't seem natural. A swirling water tornado emerged from the peak rising towards the unseen surface. As they moved closer, Danesh realized this was indeed not a natural pyramid. The sides had been formed from coral and stone and there were large entrances everywhere in the base that resembled pipes.

They avoided these, and instead swam through a triangular opening that was the start of a tunnel lit by a ghostly, blue-green glow in the walls.

Danesh leaned over to Medusa. "That portal we come through ... We in the Dreamtide or the real world?"

Bejara answered from behind, "We in a place where there ain't got no difference." The hostility in her voice made him anxious again.

The party emerged onto a ledge overlooking a long chasm that deepened going away from them. All the pipes from outside seemed to empty out of the walls of the deep space. At the deep end of the chasm, on the far side of the visibly turbulent water, stood the four sponges that made up the Parliament. Two of them stood on either side of a boulder. They were monstrous compared to the sponges Danesh had seen on the reefs, with each of these the size of a car.

One was a purple egg-shape with dimples that reminded Danesh of a breadfruit or a cactus. Another was a collection of yellow tubes that seemed to grow out of the ground. The third had formations on the outside of its round body that made it look like a neon green brain. The last was like an upside-down skirt made of lace.

"Sponge is a animal don't ever move," said Medusa. "The water bring everything to them. And this temple is where all the current from every ocean does come together and it go to the parliament, through them, and show them everything in the world."

A voice like faint gurgling spoke. "Come out/show you'self, surface son."

Danesh looked to the Apexa to confirm that meant him, then swam out. He floated in the open water above the trough where the currents mixed, the pyramid's interior walls sloping above him.

"Hello?"

Another gurgling voice. This was the pink sponge, Danesh somehow knew. "The Mark of Zadoq'ua, it there/it put pon you. But we not see evil/bad intention."

"Hope/redemption inside of you for us/you/world," said the yellow tubes.

"That can't be right," Bejara shouted. "He's a blight. He—"

"You only a guest here," Numah said pointing a finger at Bejara. "You ain't got no right fo' speak."

For a moment, Danesh thought the princess would bite Numah's finger off, she looked so savage in her hatred.

"Capabilities/secrets this one got," said the brain sponge. "Ability/probability fo' defeat/deny Zadoq'ua. To be sure of quality/usefulness, must be trial/tasks."

"You want fo' test me?" Danesh asked. "And then put me fo' fight some *crappo* monster?"

"Chance/idea only," said the pink frills. "Trial/tasks gon' show/predict."

"I ain't fighting nobody! I only come here because them people would kill me otherwise." He pointed at the council. "Is you monster. You find a way fo' beat he backside. Don't put me—"

A new voice spoke. Less gurgly and more like a rumble. "You not anything/something without knowing/earning." It took a moment for Danesh to realise the 'boulder' in the centre was actually a sponge too.

He said to it, "You saying I should do you trial for me own satisfaction?"

"Self/purpose you never have/know. Then choice/action don't got meaning/satisfaction."

Danesh thought of all the weights he had bench-pressed. All the weights he had *failed* to bench-press, no matter how hard he tried. The idea that there might be a reason to his life had only occurred to him after Medusa's attack. But it was still vague, and this trial could give him the first solid idea of who he was meant to be.

It sounded like he would fail it in any case, so he wouldn't have to worry about being some saviour for the ocean.

"Alright," he said, "When we start?"

But the sponges had gone silent. Nothing remained but the hum of rushing water.

Numah said, "When the new moon born is the time fo' trials."

"And what I gon' got fo' do? Hold me breath longer than a dolphin?"

"The moon gon' tell we that."

The next day, the people from the government finally burnt the whale carcass out of desperation. The smoke rose high and dark and the smell of acrid fuel and rotting flesh blossomed over the village like the passage of Death's Angel and then dissipated.

Despite earlier mocking the idea that he was a hero, Danesh took the cleansing of the village's atmosphere as a sign that he was on the path the Universe meant for him to be taking.

That afternoon he came home and saw his mother preparing a basin of ochro for the evening meal. Usually he would have made 'ugkh' sounds at this while pretending to choke, but his good mood could not be spoiled. He even kissed her on the cheek and jokingly asked her to make extra for him. As she worked, however, he fixed himself a snack of cheese and boiled eggs and put it away in his backpack.

His father was home today too, sitting on the upstairs balcony with *Aja*. He caught a brief exchange between them about fish prices and left. That was all they ever talked about and he had no tolerance for mundane topics today.

After he had used his sickle to cut that day's load of grass, he called up Amit on his cellphone and they met at the canal near *Aja*'s farm. As he got there a chicken hawk flew past from the grove where the old Dutch tomb lay, a toad gripped in its talons. For a moment, Danesh wanted to throw up and he stopped his bicycle to keep his balance. He spotted Surwa leaping around and barking in some tall bushes and his mind cleared up. Danesh pushed his bike over to where Amit was sharpening a cutlass as he sat on the log bridge that crossed the drainage trench.

Around them all the fields were flooded in preparation for planting, looking like rectangular lakes.

Danesh dropped his bag and sat side-by-side with Amit like they were small children, their legs dangling off the edge. The closeness didn't last long. As soon as Amit saw Danesh was about to eat eggs, he pushed him away and got up. "Boil egg does make you fart stink. What you eating all that for?"

"Protein. Muscle don't make out of air."

"You still bothering with gym?"

"You still bothering with Susie?"

Amit took a deep breath and pressed his lips together.

"Oh, sorry, man," Danesh said.

"Is alright. I just got fo' find a place to live in town. Me aunty say—"

Surwa came running up to Danesh. The dog sniffed his food and then licked his face and ran off, trying to make friends with a calf that was tied nearby as well as a few grown cows.

Danesh stood and put a hand on his friend's shoulder. "It gon' work out. Trust me."

"Yeah."

But despite his words, Danesh found it hard to sympathise with Amit. Every day for the last week he had sleep-walked through the land-world, happy memories of the deep in his head.

He remembered a few days ago when he had raced against a dolphin. He had lost horribly in the end, but just for a moment he had been at the limits of his body's capabilities, feeling like he was made of power.

He remembered when he and Medusa had played with an old leatherback turtle, rolling it over again and again and how the turtle had kept coming back so they could repeat the game.

The portals of the Dreamtide had taken him around the world – to wade in glowing, electric blue waves sweeping into a beach in Costa Rica at night. To observe polar bears from the rickety safety of ice floes off the Siberian coast. To wander the ruins of ancient temples under the North Sea.

And while he always ended up back in Essequibo, as if

falling to the bottom of a well, he knew he'd have another chance to climb up to the light again.

Seeing Surwa's failed attempts to engage the calf, Danesh removed a piece of cheese and started walking over, hand held out.

Amit said, "Calf gon' eat cheese? You mad or what?"

"Is not milk calf does drink? Well is milk cheese make with." Danesh shooed Surwa back towards Amit. The calf was tied at the end of a fifteen-foot length of rope that was secured to a wooden stake. Danesh walked about halfway out and waited for the calf to approach the proffered treat. Instead, the calf circled away. The rope was wrapping around Danesh's ankles. For a moment an image flashed in his mind of the way cows were killed at Eid – the Muslim holiday when they sacrificed bulls – by first having their feet wrapped and then pulled out from under them so they could not move. But he wasn't alarmed. The calf wasn't strong enough to bring him down and as it wound the rope around him, it would get closer and closer. And then the calf would taste the cheese and like it and they would be friends. Simple.

Except that Surwa jumped into the action when the calf had walked a full circle around Danesh and was just within reach. The dog dodged the calf's attempt at a headbutt and collided with Danesh's knees. With his ankles tied, he lost balance and fell sideways. The calf began yelling. All around the cows replied in angry bellows.

With his ankles locked together, Danesh could not stand. The calf's panicked pulling attempts to get away kept the rope taut defying Danesh's attempts to free himself.

And then the calf turned murderous. It whirled on Danesh and then reared up and brought its sharp hooves down on his ribs.

The pain spiked into his brain. He reached to restrain the calf, but it had jumped sideways and now brought the hooves down on his hip.

A great fear enveloped Danesh, something so deep he instinctively understood that it came from beyond what was happening. His mind swam with images of blood and great heaving breaths as he remembered Eid day.

Aja always had a few animals ready for sale and Danesh would take them to the new owners' pastures a week before the holiday so they could fatten up. Last year was the first time he had gone to the actual slaughterhouse, making a last-minute sale. The violence had shocked him. From the moment the ropes had been looped around their hooves and they had been dropped sideways onto the concrete, the butchers had been relentless. As each animal struggled with snorting breaths, they held the head down while the priest said some words and then one of them sawed through the skin and windpipe and jugular veins with a steel knife.

The bull's eyes had gone wide and its restrained legs had spasmed throwing some of the men off balance. Blood spurted across the wet concrete, pouring like a thick, red waterfall, then slowly ebbing away to a trickle. As the men hosed the blood away into the drains, the life of the bull slowly slipped away, the harsh sucking sound of its open windpipe fading to a whisper and its eyes going blank and still. The loss of vitality had been so final that Danesh could not imagine the bull ever being alive at all.

Without pause for dignity or reflection, the hooves were sawed off and the animal strung up on hooks at the ends of chains and a pulley. A wheelbarrow was placed to catch the entrails and the beast was gutted, then skinned. The chopping up had started by the time Danesh left, disappointed that the sacrifice had seemed so mechanical and not sacred at all.

Now, as Danesh rolled away and the calf stomped him a third time in his back, Danesh felt terror at his inability to escape. Like the bull on the concrete last year, there was nowhere for him to go.

Then the wicked little hooves stopped their stabbing. The dog ceased barking and the cows went quiet.

And he could move his feet! He scrambled upright and turned to see Amit staring at him half in alarm and half in amusement. He was holding the piece of rope he had cut away with his cutlass.

He started to utter his thanks only for pain to flood his side and he fell to his knees. The impact knocked the breath out of him and when he inhaled the flood of pain returned.

"Don't touch me," he wheezed as Amit leaned down.

"I just need you phone." He eased it out of Danesh's front pocket, and it seemed undamaged by all the stomping the calf had done. "What you got you *aja* number under?"

Aja had to arrange for a taxi-driver friend of his to take Danesh to the hospital. It turned out he had a bruised rib and he missed the next day of school but was home that night. Despite the pain medications, his chest hurt constantly and worst of all was the unexplained sense of dread that stayed with him after the attack.

He couldn't sleep and watching television late at night didn't help. He turned the screen off in frustration at about 2:00 in the morning. Over on the side wall, his mother's lit-up Om was active, sending spirals of red, green, yellow and blue outward. The pattern held his gaze and his mind felt cushioned and comforted.

He didn't remember falling asleep, but he awoke for school feeling like he'd gotten a full night's rest.

"Look, the bullfighter come!" shouted Kevitt as Danesh walked down the path from the old koker to the stretch of beach where his father's boat had been hauled up onto the sand from the channel. Amit and the other three boys laughed.

"Why you late, bullfighter?" Amit asked. "I waiting for a partner fo' play this game."

Danesh sat carefully in the boat. Even though it had been a few days, his ribs hurt as badly as ever when disturbed. He lifted

Amit's cricket bat out of the way of his legs and dropped it onto the sand.

Cricket was over for the day. Now they were playing dominoes, with an upturned equipment box as the table. They played teams, with one pair of boys sitting out a game when they lost. The six of them slammed the cheap, white dominoes on the paint-flecked wood in turn. The point of a good domino game was to make noise with the cracking impacts of the pieces as much as it was to win on points.

Over by the vines that marked the end of the rising sand, a movement caught Danesh's eye.

"Why that fish over there?" It was a small cuirass catfish, flat on its belly and almost hidden in the green.

"You *aja* been here when the boat come in," said Kevitt. He slapped his domino down. It seemed like every new game he got more violent with his play.

"Yeah," said Amit. "We help clean up, so he say we can keep the small fish and cook it tonight. We gon' fry he up over by the shed."

Danesh wasn't sure he'd be joining in. The shed meant ganja and he hadn't felt the need to smoke since discovering Coral City.

The catfish wriggled and Robot, who was not in the game, leapt out of the boat and slapped its head. "Hey," he shouted at it, then slapped it again. "You want me detain you?" He laughed and then slapped the fish with the cricket bat. "You want me detain you?"

Since his father was a policeman, Robot often used words like 'detain'.

The fish went still and Robot nodded in satisfaction. "Oh-ho."

Just as he stood, the fish shifted. This time he gave a

mighty slap with the bat to the side of the animal's head.

"Hey, watch it," Danesh shouted, you gon' damage the fish."

Too late. It had been busted open.

"He resisting arrest," Robot said, laughing, "He got fo' get beat."

"Yeah," shouted Amit. He took a piece of driftwood and shattered it across the top of the fish's back.

As Danesh watched, the other three boys joined in, and for a while the fish twisted its way down the loose sand towards the water in a swimming motion, but then the accumulated hits became too much. Even after it went still, the boys kept beating it, laughing. Kevitt even found a head-sized rock to throw at it repeatedly.

Watching the catfish die for the boys' amusement he recalled the scene from *The Lord of the Flies* where the boys had mistaken one of their own for a monster and killed him in a circle of stabbing spears on a darkened beach. They had been assigned the book last year but had found the language so dense that even Sir Karan and his poetic skills had been unable to handle it and he had given up trying to teach it after two weeks.

But the story's setup of dozens of boys stranded on an island with no adults had intrigued Danesh enough that he had downloaded the movie. The Bollywood movies he was used to were full of gangs who beat up innocent shopkeepers until the heroic police inspector would show up in his sunshades. Those gangsters were greedy and malevolent to the core and he understood their world. But the gang attack in the island movie had been so senseless that it had churned Danesh's stomach. Now he felt that same revulsion and he realized that the real evil in the world didn't come with malicious intent. He thought of the quest he'd been selected for – stopping a god – and shook his head at its futility. What this fish was to these boys was what humans were to Old Ones like Zadoq'ua.

And it wasn't just gods or boys. It was the whole world. He thought of his *Aji* Meena, his grandfather's wife, who had drowned one Sunday after slipping in the river during her morning *puja* prayer. This was a world that didn't care and where bad things happened for no good reason.

By the time Robot and the others were done with the fish, there wasn't anything worth cooking, so they left the carcass for the tide.

When Danesh arrived in Coral City for the first task, it was night. At first he didn't realise because his Clearsight was automatically on and it gave him an unhindered view. But a faint instinct made him step back and see the reality.

The seascrapers all glowed faintly blue-green in the darkness. And so did the people swimming in the space between them. Medusa's normally dark features were awash in waves of electric violet light as her *mojh* lit up the water around her. Even her hair emitted a white light.

He said, "You look..."

"What?" she asked.

The concept in his head was 'otherworldly' or 'ethereal', but he didn't have those words. Instead he said, "You look like a Samsung screensaver."

She knitted her brows and then waved him away, "I ain't know that's what. Come, we late."

Four priestesses were waiting for them in the temple which was on the top of a half-pyramid. In the centre of the wide square platform of scarred stone was a shallow, circular depression ringed by statues of tall, serene fairmaids painted in yellow and green. Bejara and the council were there too. At the bottom of the sunken space, a sponge which looked like a collection of pink pipes grew on the top of a half-column of knobby coral.

Bejara swam over and hovered in Danesh's way, her *mojh* glowing red. "Don't think that because the Parliament didn't order you fo' get execute, that I stop thinking you soul belong to Zadoq'ua. This trial is just fo' see if we can use he touch against he. That kinda thing does happen now and again. But is still the touch from a demon, so I not gon' ever trust it. Or trust you." She swung her *daki* blade slowly until it pointed at his face and then swam away.

"That lady crazy," Danesh told Medusa. She looked down, embarrassed, and said nothing.

The priestesses circled the column with long, thin vases held to their breasts like babies. Each took a cardinal point on the compass, Danesh noted, glad that his sense of direction was getting better. They unstopped the vases and pointed them at the sponge. Cloudy, green liquid poured out and stretched in a thin line to the sponge, clearly being carried by a current. The four lines converged and entered the sponge at the bottom and vanished. For a half-minute. It emerged from the top, like green steam. The priestesses pressed their faces in and breathed it all in. Their eyes fluttered and they went still.

The chief priestess cleared her throat and spoke, eyes still closed. "Danesh from the surface world, for the first task in you trial you must travel to the island of Polyphemus the Cyclops and take the thing which he love the most."

Danesh waited, but the priestesses simply continued to drift in a slow circle around the green cloud that was forming.

"I got fo' get more direction than that," he said to the Apexa.

"Medusa gon' show you where," said Numah. "But she can't interfere. The Parliament gon' know if you cheat."

"But I ain't know anything about Poly-whoever. I mean, they can't tell me if I got fo' thief he shoes or he motorbike or what?"

"All that is part of the trial," said the Apexa. "If you can know the answer, then you's the person we looking for."

"Is not fair!"

Ignoring him, the council swam away.

He turned to Medusa. "Is not fair..."

"Polyphemus is the monster that eat Odysseus men when they get shipwreck," said Medusa as they swam away from Coral City. "Remember we hear the story last week? How they stick a big timber in the Cyclops one eye and blind he?"

"Yeah, I just didn't knew the name is all," said Danesh in annoyance.

Medusa was pulling something behind her that looked like a chariot, except the compartment was an egg-shaped bubble of steel and *mojh*. It was light enough to float with them.

The *ummbb* of the portal sang them through to the other side into daylight. The island about three miles away had a bright, sandy beach in a curved bay backed by tall date palms and rocky cliffs.

Danesh scoured the tops of the cliffs for a sighting. "This Polyphemus does look after sheep, right?

"Right."

"And in the story, he take care of them even after he get blind, right?"

"Yeah," said Medusa, looking puzzled.

"Then I think the thing he love the most got fo' be he sheep. A sheep can live in that egg?"

"Yes. For a whole day even."

"Let me get some of that rope you got."

Medusa gave him two lengths of the rope, each about ten feet long. She showed him the tap codes for the metal ends that made them loosen and tighten.

"Is how strong is this?" Danesh asked.

"Strong. It make out of a special seaweed and sponge and coral."

"I can join the metal parts together?"

She showed him the tap code for that. The pieces of metal seemed to fuse into each other. "You can join more than two even."

"Really?" He raised an eyebrow. "You sure you don't got more rope?"

She narrowed her eyes at him and then grudgingly brought out another length.

"Ah," said Danesh, "Perfect. Let we go."

"I can't come more close."

"Oh, right."

He swam carefully to the beach, pulling the egg carriage and keeping an eye out below and above the water. Unfortunately, his Clearsight didn't let him see past the trees at the base of the cliff. He also kept his speed down because exertion made his ribs hurt.

When he was about halfway in, a deep voice spoke to his right. "A man don't always know what he love, but he always show what he love from how he behave."

Danesh turned to see the curved beak of a great turtle. The animal was twice his length and he couldn't believe it had gotten so close without him knowing. And, of course, he couldn't believe it was talking to him.

He asked, "Who's you?"

The turtle's back fins kicked lazily but gave it enormous speed, and it glided past Danesh.

He chased it. "Hey, what you doing here?"

"I just talking. Nobody can't help you, Danesh, but the rule don't say I can't talk."

"So what you want talk about?"

"Love."

"I don't know nothing about love. I think I like this one girl a lot, but she from a different world and–"

"Not about you!"

"Oh. Sorry."

"I talking about this test. The other thing you got fo' remember is that what a man love fo' do, is not what he do the most."

Then the great turtle banked away, showing its pale pink belly against its green shell.

Danesh had reached the island. He left the egg in the shallow water then held himself low and walked up the beach. In the tree line, he felt safer and began to climb one of the date trees.

A crashing in the undergrowth made him freeze. The sheep were coming, a massive herd of them, creating more noise. There were mighty rams with curved brown horns and mothers with lambs hopping along behind. Danesh watched the hundreds of sheep wander into the trees, eating the grass there. A lone, young sheep passed near him.

Still no sign of the one-eyed giant. This was too good a chance. He dropped onto the back of the animal and held on to its sides. He drew one of the lengths of rope tight around the sheep's woolly neck and it was his. It began bleating loudly, and Danesh climbed off and started pulling it towards the water. The sheep was stronger than it looked, and Danesh had to dig his feet into the sand to get it over to the carriage. His palms were burning from the pull of the rope.

He tapped the code to unlock the egg and pushed the top half open. A bellow of rage rang out from the cliff top. With the strength of panic, Danesh lifted the sheep and dumped it into the carriage.

A boulder splashed into the sea next to him, sending up a shower of sand and misty water. A group of four more boulders landed deeper in the ocean right after. The cyclops might be blind, but he could hear the sheep's cries. Danesh pushed the sheep deeper into its compartment so he could bring the lid down. Just then, a boulder landed on the lid and slammed it onto his elbow.

He landed in the water, gritting his teeth and holding his arm. The egg was only dented he saw to his relief. And the impact had scared the sheep so much it had stopped trying to escape, though it was still bleating at top volume. Danesh reached up with his good hand, making his rib explode in pain, and shut the compartment.

The sound of the frightened sheep did not lessen much. And now the distinct thuds of the blind giant's approach shook the beach.

The monster was five times Danesh's height, with thickly muscled legs. It held a club that was actually an uprooted tree – Danesh could see where the branches had been cut off to leave spikes. Aside from that, and the massive scarred eye of course, the cyclops looked very much like a shepherd, with a leather bag hung over his shoulder and a skirt of fur around his waist.

If Danesh ran away, he would lose the sheep. If he stayed, he would be caught and probably eaten.

There was only one other choice. He ran toward the giant, joining his remaining two ropes into one extra-long piece. As one massive foot – it was the size of a wheelbarrow – landed on the ground near him, he leapt onto it and wrapped the rope around the ankle before securing the free metal end back to the join in the centre. One half of his 'handcuffs' were complete.

The giant slowed his step to grab at Danesh and he jumped off, the impact jarring his pained ribs. He breathed in as deeply as he could manage without straining his chest too much and took this chance to get onto the giant's other foot, still holding the free end of the rope. By the time he had looped this end around and joined it to the centre, the giant was reaching for him again and this time got him by the legs. Just as he felt the great fingers begin to squeeze, Danesh finished tapping the code for tightening the rope and it snapped the two oversized ankles together. The impact shook him free and he scrambled away, holding his side.

With a sense of slow inevitability, the one-eyed monster swayed and fell face first into the water, roaring all the way. It splashed into water deep enough to cover its head when it landed and it sputtered and tried to get up. One flailing hand reached down and pushed it up. Another grabbed the egg with the sheep inside and held it.

But being blind and hobbled by the rope, the creature was having a hard time getting up. And like a giant toddler it kept trying to free the sheep instead of devoting its energies to rising. For the first time Danesh got a sense that Polyphemus was lacking some specific mental power.

But the giant's confusion would not last long. As Danesh saw it, he either had to leave the sheep behind in the giant's hands or pull the creature out to sea. Danesh had spent enough time in the ocean to know that Zadoq'ua's touch gave him super-strength when he was in the water. If he got Polyphemus deep enough, the giant would drown, and the sheep would be Danesh's.

The image of being unable to breathe while tied up broke into Danesh's mind and reignited that feeling of ultimate dread that he had first suffered during the calf attack.

This thing with Polyphemus had gotten out of hand. He didn't care what the Parliament of Sponges said, he couldn't put anyone through that again.

Again? What do I mean ag–

Danesh saw Medusa looking at him from the beyond the breaking waves. Felt her more like. He signalled her to stay away and approached the monster, getting right up to the water's edge.

"Excuse me!" he shouted. "We can talk?"

The giant turned his one dead eye in Danesh's direction and roared out a blast of warm, foul air.

Danesh said, "If I loose you, you promise you not gon' hurt me?"

"I gon' break you in half no matter what! This weak trap ain't gon' hold me. I gon' get out. And then I gon' ram a boulder right up you–"

"Yeah, yeah, I understand all that, but I asking you if we can't do it a different way. I let you out and both of we gon' go we own way in peace and never talk about it, like it never happen."

The giant looked sightlessly up at the cliffs. "You promise?"

"Yes."

"You not gon' tell me brothers?" This was an opportunity, Danesh realized. The cyclops cared about his brothers' opinions, it seemed.

"I not gon' tell them," Danesh said. "Especially not them."

The giant thought about it then said, "You got fo' give me back me sheep, too." He held out the egg-shaped prison.

"But I need it for something import–"

"Is *my* sheep!"

Images from long ago of the drunk old man looking for his

stolen bike came back to Danesh. "Yeah," he said to Polyphemus, "you right. I gon' give it back."

"Good." Polyphemus relaxed, sitting upright in the water.

"I gon' loose the rope now," Danesh called up to him. He tapped for the release and the joined rope separated and fell. Terrified that the giant might change his mind, Danesh held still for a moment, prepared to run for the trees.

The giant simply stood and walked onto the beach. Danesh picked up his ropes and followed. In the dry, loose sand above the high tide line, Polyphemus sat cross-legged and put the egg with the now gently bleating sheep down before him. "Open this thing now."

"Yes, sure." Danesh tapped the lid open and the sheep bounded out, running straight into the shepherd's giant lap. Polyphemus stroked its neck and back like a kitten. In fact, it was the size of a kitten compared to the giant.

"I sorry about this," said Danesh. "I trying fo' do something good, but I make a mistake."

Polyphemus didn't answer. He just took a deep breath and kept petting his sheep.

Danesh said, "You got very nice sheep."

"They's the only ones who like me."

"I like you." Danesh wasn't sure why he said that, but realised immediately that it was true.

"Really?"

"Well, I like you *now*. Not when you been trying fo' kill me. You just protecting you sheep. I understand. I does take care of cows back home." He didn't mention what usually became of the cows.

"Li'l man," said the giant, "Don't bother me no more. You say you woulda leave after you free me."

"Yeah, but I don't really got nowhere fo' go. I can't stay

here li'l bit?"

"You ain't got no home?"

"Yeah, but it give me stress, you know?"

"Mhmm."

After the giant stayed silent for a while, Danesh decided to see what Polyphemus's view on the old story about himself was. He asked, "So what happened to your eye?"

"Odysseus."

"What's that? A disease?"

The cyclops laughed bitterly. "Close. He was a man. You never hear about he?"

"No." Danesh said, continuing the deception. "He famous? Like a singer or something?"

"He? Sing? No talent. No ear. But he famous, yes." Polyphemus leaned back on his arm and his fingers brushed one of the many boulders he had thrown down from the cliff top earlier. "Everyone know about how Odysseus clever. Smartest man in the whole Greek army."

"Well you ain't got fo' be afraid of me. I stupid. They even make me go to a school for stupid people."

"My brothers call me stupid. Even my father. Because Odysseus play a word trick game pon me and make me tell them that 'nobody' blind me after he stick a pole in me eye." The cyclops picked up the boulder and threw it like a pebble into the bay. "Nobody don't think I can ever do anything clever."

"Yeah. I know what you mean." Danesh shrugged. "Except drumming. Everybody at the temple know I can play the drum good."

Polyphemus smiled. "You like music? Let me show you something."

From his bag, he drew up a flute made of pipes that had been tied side-by-side, longest to shortest. "This here is me

122

syrinx." He put it to his lips and a calming sound washed over Danesh, making him feel like he was bathing in the wind. The flute must have been as wide as Danesh's arm span, but with his large hands the cyclops played it nimbly, moving it side to side to vary the pitch of the notes and sometimes shaking the whole thing carefully to make the music seem to vibrate.

The melody was a little sad, but also sweet. Polyphemus played with his eye closed, head and neck swaying as if he was floating on his own music. The sheep started coming out of the trees to hear the music. By the end of the song, about thirty of them were on the sand, looking up at their master.

"That's some good playing, boss. You sound like you put you soul into it."

"Is practice," said Polyphemus, with pride. "It hard fo' do. You know, my brothers make fun of me when I been learning and I didn't sound so good. But I love the sounds I make with the flute. It feel like the flute begging me fo' play it, so I used to hide from me brothers and play. And now they know I can play good, they ask me for music all the time, but I don't play when I around them. I play for me."

"Polyphemus," Danesh said hesitantly, "if I tell you I need that syrinx for something really important, you would let me take it?"

"How important?"

Danesh started telling him about meeting Medusa and how it led to finding out about Zadoq'ua.

"Oh, this is fo' impress a girl," laughed Polyphemus. "Well, no problem then. Things gon' be quiet 'til I make a new one, but you's the nicest thief I ever meet, so I don't mind too much."

Danesh was just about to object that this wasn't about Medusa at all when he realised he was getting exactly what he wanted, so he clamped his teeth together.

An hour later, he and Medusa were back in Coral City with the flute – the thing Polyphemus loved most – packed safely in the egg-box.

Bejara watched suspiciously as they handed it over to the council. "No way a boy like you figure out the trick by you'self. You sure you didn't cheat?"

"I just talk nice to the big man. You should try being nice to people sometimes and see if they don't like you more." He decided not to mention the turtle who had spoken to him.

Bejara gritted her teeth with outrage, but before she could say anything more, Numah interrupted.

"We gon' send this to the Parliament of Sponges," he told Danesh. "They send you fo' get it for a reason, not just fo' give you something hard to do. They gon' know the best use for it."

He awoke in his room to hammering downstairs. It was dark still. He wondered briefly what his father was making noise for, but his thoughts soon gathered around the happy memory of what he had accomplished. He'd succeeded at a quest. Like a real hero. Living in a great uncaring universe dominated by creatures like Zadoq'ua no longer seemed like a hopeless situation.

More pounding. Someone was at the door. He got up, already eager to run through his day. He would even smile and say good morning to Miss Geeta and mean it.

He reached the kitchen just in time to see one of Amit's cousins leaving. Danesh's mother looked at him with sympathy. "Amit drink poison last night. He dead at the hospital before the doctor could arrive."

Danesh said nothing, searching her face to see if this could be a prank. But she never made those kinds of jokes. He sat at the old table with its faded, blue paint, stunned by the fact that the best reason to believe Amit had really died was how *normal* this scene was. His whole life, there had been meals a couple of times a year where the news of someone drinking poison would come up, usually followed by who they had 'drunk it for' – that is, who they had been in love with and been unable to attain.

It had almost been a joke. He remembered as a child laughing at one story of a neighbor whose ten-year-old son had saved his life by feeding him raw eggs until he threw up the poison.

"That boy, Amit," said his mother now. "I can't believe he do this to he parents. They work so hard fo' raise he and he so ungrateful, I can't–"

"Don't say that!"

"Is true!"

"No." He thought of what the doctor had said at the school assembly. "There ain't got nobody fo' blame. The people who do this, they just suffering is all."

"Everybody suffer. That don't mean they got fo' kill theyself. You think living with you father easy? He used fo' work boat for one month and then drink rum for one month straight. If wasn't for you *Aja* putting he in order..."

He wanted to defend Amit. He knew suicide wasn't about people being weak or not valuing their lives or any of the things people normally said, but he was angry. Amit had gone and done the most final thing a person could do. And left Danesh alone. Without even saying anything. He had no words for what he felt, but it reminded him of times when he got picked last for a cricket team or when Miss Geeta had made fun of his reading.

Danesh got up and dressed without his normal shower then left his breakfast behind and went to school.

By the time of the funeral two days later, Danesh was still not sure what he felt. Having time to reflect had given him guilt of his own. He should have acted more impressed with the fireworks. He should have talked to Susie's parents about Amit. He should have *known* that his best friend was thinking of killing himself.

And while all those feelings were whirling around in a hurricane, Danesh was avoiding the most serious and destructive winds near the centre of his emotions: his best friend had been taken away and it felt *wrong*.

At Miss Geeta's urging, the principal had refused to sanction Danesh and the other students going to the cremation in uniform with a teacher because Amit was technically no longer a student. Danesh, Robot, Kevitt, Nadira and a few others left after lunch anyway and took up a position to one side of the observation stand, near the ocean.

On the wide strip of sand before the stand, a head-high pyre had been constructed from thick, industrial firewood stacked upright around a central platform. The pandit circled it, preparing the wood with flammable *ghee* and saying prayers.

As Danesh waited in choked silence, the others quietly bantered behind him. He understood that they didn't mean disrespect, but it frustrated him to think that they weren't as paralysed by Amit's passing as he was.

"Something wrong with coolie people," Robot said. "Is only they does kill out they self like this."

He had a point. The doctor's numbers said it was mostly Indians who committed suicide.

"Wait," said Kevitt, "Robot, you not half Indian?"

"Yeah, so?"

"You better watch out," Nadira said, "or you coolie half might kill you black half."

The students all snickered. Even Danesh. Amit would have enjoyed that joke.

But Amit wasn't here. He was gone. A victim of an absurd world not built for human needs.

The pickup truck with Amit's body reversed up the dirt track to the cremation ground. His father, uncles and cousins took charge, removing his bier, which was made of bamboo ribs covered in white cotton and hung with hibiscus flowers and yellow ribbons.

More prayers followed. In the crowd, Danesh saw *Aja* and Jones. Most of the onlookers, however, had no real connection to Amit. They were neighbors and friends of his family. A part of Danesh felt like they didn't deserve to be there. How could they mourn if they didn't even know what the world had lost with Amit's death?

The pandit put a lit torch to the wood in three places. The fuel kept the flames going until the wood caught fire and thick, soupy, smoke billowed westward in the ocean wind. The fire grew slowly at first, but soon became a tall pillar of flame, sending heat hundreds of feet in all directions and making Danesh sweat. The white bier and its flowers turned black and disappeared within the blaze.

Jones walked over to Danesh and put a hand on his shoulder. "I know this is a hard time for you, but I need fo' tell you, I hope what you see here today make you understand you can't waste you life."

"What you talking about?"

"Young people in this place, in Essequibo, they don't got ambition. They don't work to make theyself better because they can't see no better. *You* different. You got skills and hope and you can–"

Danesh pushed himself away. "Ain't nothing like hope in this world."

Jones looked exasperated. "You wrong, there–"

"Man, stop talking like some teacher and trying fo' tell me how fo' live me life." He turned away and walked to the edge of the ocean. Out there was a city of wonder, an amazing girl, and a limitless world of possibilities. All worthless and inconsequential.

"You can't be vex with Jones," said *Aja* walking up behind him. The old man looked serious and sad.

"I thought you was supposed fo' go to the bush yesterday."

"Amit been almost like another grandson to me. Diamond bush can wait a couple more day."

Danesh nodded, grateful that someone seemed to understand the loss that had taken place.

"But Amit gone," said *Aja*, "and you still here. So remember, it don't matter how bad the world get, there always a way fo' win. If nothing else I teach you in this life, remember that. There always got some way – some opening – fo' get back what belong to you."

He kissed Danesh on the top of his head and left, walking to the main road where he caught a taxi.

He was called into the principal's office the next morning. Miss Geeta wanted him suspended for flagrant disobedience. Miss Corrine told her to calm down and have some sympathy.

"Danesh," she said, "I know you lost your friend and that can't be easy, but..."

He turned and walked out. The two teachers shouted for him to come back, but he saw no reason to stay there within the school's walls anymore. Amit had walked away from all this. Why shouldn't he? The guard snoozing at the school gate awoke too late to stop him, and he headed for the backdam.

He spent the day numb. He found the cow *Aja* had left in his care at its grazing spot and set it loose. His grandfather's other two cows had been sold to the butcher before he left. Danesh wondered at the pointlessness of this cow's life. It too was destined to die under a butcher's knife.

By afternoon, he still had not eaten anything. The first bite he took of a guava he had picked near the Dutch Man Tomb nauseated him and he'd tossed it away.

Night found him in the smoke shed, which was an abandoned watchman's shack near the koker. The roof had blown off some time ago and the village boys had replaced it with old tarpaulins. The front windows were gone too, but that only gave a better view of the ocean, so they had left them that way.

The regular smokers showed up after their dinner. These were mostly older teens, but they were friendly enough with Danesh to share their weed with him. He soon lost track of time. The world shrank inward to just him and his memories and his desires. And none of those three things seemed solid or reliable.

He didn't know what he wanted from life. Did he want anything at all? Time stretched in all directions around him. The faces of the other teens in the hut showed dark and distorted.

Then the bell started.

It was a faint chime, but soon it became the only thing he could hear. No one else was reacting so the call was in his head it seemed. Danesh swayed to his feet. Someone laughed at him. He ignored it and staggered out into the open air.

His Clearsight was on, but it wasn't the ocean he saw. Instead, a path stretched through the midnight land. It illuminated the grass down the bank of the sea dam and across the narrow planks which made a bridge over the drainage ditch.

Then it stretched straight down the village street, across the main road and down into the backdam. And the bonging of the bell was coming from there.

Danesh answered, walking in a continued daze, his sense of time falling in and out of synch with his steps.

Near *Aja's* farm, the path turned left, straight to the old tomb. He stepped over the low wrought iron fence that ringed the curved stone and cement construct. The path he could see with his Clearsight ended with three glowing spots on the rough surface. He tapped them, instinctively knowing the order.

Lines of sickly yellow light broke through the top of the tomb and the surface rolled open. Small, clammy shapes bumped his bare legs and the flickering light from inside revealed a dozen or so brown *crappos* hopping out of the entrance. Inside the doors, stairs led downward, too deep for Danesh to see the bottom. But there was light down there and he could hear the bell calling from underground.

With his feet still unsteady, he braced against the wall and descended. The surfaces here were pure stone, not the cement that had been used above. Each shimmery ring of the bell echoed up and down the enclosed stairway.

Eventually, Danesh got to a point where the distance back up seemed just as far as the distance to the unseen bottom. The air smelled like wet tree roots. He continued down.

The stairs grew wider and the ceiling of the stairwell grew taller until Danesh found himself descending into an open hall as large as a cathedral. The walls were lined with drains and alcoves. The central space was full of ancient stone benches focused on a stage with a podium on it. The room was lit as if by golden fire, but every time Danesh turned to see which light was casting his shadow on the wall, all he found was another shadow.

As he crossed the hall, he saw familiar pieces of his own

world scattered at the edges of the aisle: rum bottles, rope, the buoy from a fishing net, the disc from a tractor plough, even an old shoe.

The podium was criss-crossed by beams of light whose source Danesh could not see. At their intersection lay an old book, its pages open. The writing was faded, brown ink on yellowed parchment and the language was not English. A metal plate fifteen feet tall stood behind the podium, engraved with an image of Zadoq'ua dangling a man over his broad mouth as his tongue reached up.

Danesh could still hear the clanging of the bell, but he saw no indication of where it was coming from. He looked down at the book.

Definitely not English.

But that one letter looked familiar. Something told him it produced a 'th' sound, but the same problem Danesh had with letters above came back to him here. He could not seem to hold the shape of the writing in his mind.

He looked away and noticed a small stone idol to the right of the book. It was crudely carved, but the figure was undoubtedly Zadoq'ua. Danesh picked it up and the wall plate split down the middle with a train of cracking sounds and opened. The bell clanged from within.

The revealed chamber was the opposite of grand. It was like a large grave, with sides of bare wet dirt. But that was where the bell was calling from. Danesh walked in.

In Danesh's hand, the idol grew damp and clammy. All around, the muddy walls of the hole became blurred and faded out of reality.

A cold flicker across the top of his thumb left spit on his skin. Had the idol *licked* him?

Ugh.

He managed to keep his grip on the ugly little thing, however. It seemed to be grinning at him. He said to it, "I don't care what you try. I ain't letting you go."

From the dark that now encompassed him, a growling, but almost musical, voice answered. "The question is, who hold who in their power?"

A feeling like a gaint hand closed around his body. A shivering sensation took hold of Danesh, as if the top of his head were open and a giant, slimy tongue were licking his brain.

"Stop that!" he shouted, crouching down and holding his hair. He felt giant fingers tighten around his chest and lift him into the air. His ribs seemed to pop inward as he lost his breath.

"You're not the only one that can play with carvings, little boy."

Danesh opened his eyes. The idol was a squirming, breathing thing in his hand and his Clearsight kicked in showing that Danesh was himself being held by a giant Zadoq'ua. And that Zadoq'ua was being held by a larger version of Danesh ... and so on, up and down into infinity. Dizzy, he shook his head until it was free of the image.

He still felt vulnerable, but managed to ask, "You make some kind of voodoo doll fo' torture me?"

"I make a link so that me and you can talk man-to-man even though I far away right now."

Danesh laughed. "Yeah. *Man*-to-*man*."

"We equal enough fo' call it that."

"Equal? But you's..."

"A god?"

"A monster."

Danesh sensed Zadoq'ua lean back in whichever faraway lair his real body was resting.

"To a shrimp," said the great toad, "*you's* a god and a monster. He can't imagine that even you get humble and cry tears when you realise you own insignificance in the universe."

"So, you saying that you get lonely just like people? That's why you calling me on you magic cellphone? You need a friend"

Zadoq'ua scoffed, "Lonely? I done had more friends and lovers and children than all the stars in the sky. I does wish I could be *more alone* for all they bother me. The problem don't never be loneliness. The problem is meaning."

Danesh was feeling even more dizzy now. The deep, unbroken darkness destroyed his sense of direction. Concepts like 'in' or 'up' no longer made sense.

"One of me old disciples, Eibon, he write in he book that all human thinking, all religion, all science, was like holding a candle to the night of the universe. The funny thing about that is that he look to me for illumination but is the same candle I got fo' keep back the dark."

As he thrust his hand in his pocket for his lighter, Danesh tried to focus on where the toad's voice was coming from. It gave his mind an anchor in the disorientation of the illusions. When

Zadoq'ua did not speak again, he said, "Well, it look like the dark winning."

Danesh snapped on the lighter, but Zadoq'ua had already ignited golden flames in wide, brass-ringed holes on each side of him. Even squatting on his fat hind legs, the creature was taller than a house. Or at least the image it chose to show was. Its slick skin looked leaky and soft under the glow of the fires.

The ground they stood on was grey rock, carved with lines and strange language that spread away to the horizon. In some places the writing looked rubbed out and written over. In others, faint. And a few sections had been burned into permanent scars.

"I thought..." Danesh stammered. "They tell me you live in a mud pit."

"Oh, that's true. What you see is only a corner that I does keep clean. And the power fo' create rock from mud is just one secret I learn in three billion years pon this planet."

"Three billi—"

"You ain't comprehend the *totalness* of the cosmic darkness." Zadoq'ua shook his head slowly in frustration. "Even a Great Old One like me, I does struggle fo' figure out a purpose for me life. In all this time I been pon Earth, I sometimes does decide fo' rule this planet, sometimes fo' wipe all the life clean. There got times I reward my worshipers for what they sacrifice to me and then sometimes I inflict pain pon them for spite. But more and more I find that is the time down here fighting against the unknown that's the most rewarding. Learning is the purpose fo' me life. I feeding the flame of knowledge and that holding back the eternal darkness."

Danesh shivered at the idea of sitting in Miss Geeta's class forever, learning. "Not me, boss. That sound boring as—"

"Ignorance is boring. Learning, that's motion."

"So that's why you got me here," Danesh said, his mind

clearer now that he could see. "You want fo' learn 'bout me. You know I training fo' stop you."

"And already you done show me so much."

"But if all you want is fo' stay down in you cave and study the universe, why bother with invading and killing?"

"There got other gods on this globe who fighting for power with me. Once in a while I does got fo' rise up and remind them fo' stay clear from my plans."

"And why you don't just squeeze that doll to dust in your hand and finish with me?"

"Because you purpose is not fo' beat me. Is fo' enable me." Zadoq'ua laughed his deep musical laugh.

"What you mean by that?" The idol Danesh held had become a real toad now, squirming so much he needed both hands to keep it clamped in his grasp. He shouted again at the toad god, but the walls of the farthest chamber in the Dutch Man Tomb began to lock back into reality until it was just him in the sour smell of the dirt.

His first instinct was to throw the now live toad idol into the wall, but the sense of panic was so familiar that his mind paused. It reminded him of when he had been tied up and attacked by the calf, the worst terror of his life. That had ended when he had stared into the red, blue, green, and yellow lights of his mother's Om decoration. Danesh brought up that image again, breathing deeply.

When he opened his eyes, the toad idol was just a piece of stone again. The clanging bell, the disorientation, the sense of horror were all gone.

He closed the big book on the podium and tucked it under his arm. He hauled it up the narrow stairs to the surface. When the tomb door slammed down into place, there was no mark visible for him to unlock it, no matter how hard he looked with his Clearsight.

Not that he ever wanted to go back down there again.

Two nights later, with the village quiet under the still air, he awoke to see Medusa climbing through the window.

He rubbed his eyes. "How you able fo' climb that–"

"With this." She held up her hand, showing that the *mojh* had extended from her fingertips to form luminescent claws an inch long. He'd seen her use the living substance to form webbing between her fingers when she swam, but this lethal potential was new to him. "You ain't come to visit for a long time," she said. "The priestess say you got a new quest. You got fo' go collect the Tablet of Destinies from Sedna, the queen of–"

"I ain't going."

"You got fo' go!" She pulled him upright by the arm.

"I ain't got fo' do nothing." He freed himself with an annoyed twist of his shoulder. "And it don't make no difference anyhow. We can't win."

"What wrong with you?"

"Nothing." He sat on his bed, looking out the window

at the ocean. Medusa watched him with disgust and then her expression softened to suspicion. He looked away from her, but she kept demanding answers with her expression.

Finally, he spoke. "Amit kill he'self."

"You friend? The one who love the girl he can't get?"

"Yeah. Now he won't ever get she. It don't make no difference that he dead because she still gon' live she life the same. And it don't make no difference if I live or I dead or anybody dead because the world don't care what we do."

Medusa took his hand in hers. The claws had pulled back and she held him reassuringly. "I don't know what you seeing in you future, but I got a job fo' do. And that job is fo' take you back. You want fo' be boring and sour, you can be boring and sour with me, but you can't stay here."

She removed a length of rope, tapped the metal end so that it formed a hook and then secured the rope outside his window.

He pointed to the hallway. "I can just go through the front door you know."

The ice palace where the sea goddess Sedna lived was in the north, floating in the open ocean. Its entrance was a great cave, set back from the edge of an ice shelf.

"I not going through there," Danesh said as they floated a half-mile away where the portal had deposited them. A dozen or so polar bears were wandering the path to the front door.

"Maybe you can get in from the back?" Medusa said. "Or from underneath?"

"Okay, we can swim around and–"

"I can't go. You–"

"Right, right. I got fo' go alone."

Danesh swam under the ice. He could feel the chill of the shadowy, blue water, but it didn't bother him the way freezing water should. The mark of Zadoq'ua protected him. And that made him worry. The toad god had said Danesh was somehow enabling his coming triumph. Suppose this quest was helping to destroy the world somehow?

The palace's lower surfaces looked creamy in texture, like white foam that had flowed in random directions. He touched it and found it to be quite solid, however. The curves of the ice walls, extending down, created massive spaces that dwarfed any building Danesh had ever been in. But smaller, tighter spaces were hidden in the folds of the ice walls.

None led him to an entrance.

"You can't always look with your eyes," said a familiar voice next to him.

He turned to see the great turtle. Except something about the way the light reflected down here made it seem like he could make out the faint image of a man riding the turtle.

"You come fo' talk, turtle man?"

"If you gon' listen."

"Last time I listen and it help me, so let me hear what you

got fo' say this time."

"You know the story about how the world come to be, how there didn't have nothing but a dark ocean and then the sound of creation spread through everywhere, the sacred syllable of 'Om,' and the world come out of it?"

"Yeah, the pandit talk about it in the temple sometimes."

"Sound come before light in the world. But we mistake light for reality. Remember, 'The wise behold with their mind'." Then the turtle and its ghostly rider were gone, descending into the murk.

It took a little while longer of poking about with no success before an idea occurred to Danesh. If he couldn't trust light, he would close his eyes. He drifted, his limbs loose, and let the water's flow speak to him. Felt its push and moved with it. Its murmur filled his ears, rising from a slow rumble to a faster swooshing.

Danesh felt himself carried along, tumbling, until his foot brushed something solid. He opened his eyes to see the ocean vanishing behind him as he was pulled backwards into a tunnel and washed upward into a river running through an ice cave.

He kicked for the shore and climbed out. A quick look around revealed no bears, but he walked as stealthily as he could anyway, up the sloping bank to a passage whose sides were smooth and reflective as mirrors.

The path led to a wide space where the high walls were cut into mirrored facets, like the surface of a diamond. Only the floor and ceiling remained white to reveal what was solid and real.

At the far end of the room, Medusa emerged, her *daki* held ready for a fight.

"I thought you say you can't come and help me," Danesh taunted her. "What happen, you get lost?"

She didn't answer. Instead, she drew her arm back

and sent the spear flying at his head. He ducked, the sudden movement causing a twinge in his injured ribs. The spear sunk into the mirror behind him, entering without breaking anything and disappearing. It popped cleanly out of another mirror wall to the side of him and fell into the centre of the chamber.

He ran to pick it up. So did Medusa. As they converged, the mirrors created the illusion of a hundred Medusas running towards him. He lost track of which was the real one, but one of them grabbed him in her clawed hand and threw him into a corner, knocking the air out of his lungs and making his ribs burn. He propped himself up and noticed three bleeding scratches on his arm.

In the mirrored confusion around him, the reflections separated, each acting on its own now. They were like holograms, no longer bound to the surface that had given them birth – each stabbing at him with a spear. He dodged and dodged, each motion making him wince with shooting pain in his chest. Sometimes he would be too late in his evasion, but the spear blade would glide through him harmlessly and he would realize that it wasn't real. At other times he would feel the rush of air as he almost took a hit.

But sooner or later, the real blade would strike him. He was starting to pant and move slower.

As he listened to his breathing, trying to calm it, he realized there was a slight rumbling sound that would come before one of the mirror figures struck at him. He kept track and noticed that it was always the same Medusa who produced the sound.

He stopped moving. All the other Medusas stabbed their phantom spears through him as he watched the one who had made the sound. She grinned with triumph and brought her spear down from a height. He dodged when he heard the rumble and grabbed the *daki* handle, yanking it away with one hand and grasping her wrist with the other and wrenching her to the ground.

All the attackers flickered out of existence except the Medusa whose spear he had stolen. But it wasn't Medusa. It was a wrinkled woman in brown rags, her hair grey with age.

For a moment, Danesh's grip loosened, afraid he might hurt her. Then he held her tight again. "You ... You's Sedna?"

She smiled and stood, no longer old, but a woman in her prime, her hair like flowing dark water, skin like blue ice and her clothes of brilliant green seaweed.

"I got what you come for," she said, her voice mellow and welcoming.

"Well good, because I don't even know what I come for. All I know is you supposed to be some sea goddess with a computer."

"A computer?"

"Some tablet with destiny?"

"The Tablet of Destinies is an ancient stone where we record human reality."

She pulled her wrist away from him and he reluctantly let go. She led him down the way she had first arrived and Danesh sensed no more trickery. In the next room, a column of water flowed up through the centre, as if by magic. It had to be magic. This was the house of a goddess after all.

Floating within the water was a flat stone tablet, its surface etched in angular writing.

"I just take it?" he asked, his arm halfway to the surface of the vertical stream.

"You could."

"Or?"

She raised an eyebrow. "Or you could learn."

"Is what's this thing really?"

"You know why humanity on this Earth?"

"The story I hear in Coral City is that we used to be like servants or pets for the Old Ones. But by accident we get smart and take over when they went away."

"Not smart. Conscious." She waved her hand and the room faded, just like when he'd been in Zadoq'ua's den under the Dutch Man Tomb, to reveal a vision of another time and place. A creature who resembled a man, but with the face of a reptile was carving a small stone in a temple. The shape that emerged was a grinning little toad, the same idol that had been in the tomb.

"How long ago is this?"

"Not long," said Sedna at his side. "Less than a million years."

The scene showed the reptilian's civilization worshiping Zadoq'ua. Sometimes, their cities were rich and beautiful. Sometimes, inky creatures like knife-edged shadows would emerge from the altars and lay waste the country.

Cities of men emerged, worshiping different gods and the temples of Zadoq'ua sank into the ground, forgotten, except for a loyal few who kept faith. Humans in dark corners took up his worship too, making sacrifices of animals and people before great black stones in his name.

The carved toad idol sat alone in one such temple, until the modern age. New men came to live in the land. The idol called to them too. New cultists worshiped him in their robes, using the terrible rites of blood. Right down to Danesh's time when he could see a handful of men from his own village descending into the hidden temple. Their faces were covered by their hoods, but he had no doubt that a cult of Zadoq'ua existed amid his mundane community of farmers and teachers and loggers.

A new vision grew into his mind: a celestial palace atop

a mountain that floated in a dark river of clouds that swept by without pause.

In the highest tower, a man and boy sat cross-legged facing each other and drinking tea. The man was blue-skinned, wearing gold robes and a pointed crown. Two great pointed teeth showed behind his lips. By his side sat two white hunting dogs, their eyes red and glowing.

The scene was unmistakable to Danesh – Yama, the god of death, and Nachiteka. It was from one of his favourite stories about a boy who came to find out the truth about the world beyond death. Danesh had found the answers in the original story vague, but he loved the idea of a boy who challenged a god.

But this boy was not Nachiteka. Amit sat there, his tea untouched, arguing with Yama. And while Nachiteka had come humble, ready to be the perfect pupil, Amit was defiant.

"You don't understand," the boy said to the god. "Life ain't always easy. If I can get a chance to reincarnate into a better life, why I shouldn't take it? What's the point suffering all them years?"

"You got one choice in life," said the god, sipping from his dark stone cup. "Chase what's right or chase what's pleasurable."

"I not talking 'bout pleasure. I talking about pain."

"Pain is just what we call it when we don't got pleasure. And for the people who chase pleasure, pain does make life unbearable. But if you chase what's right, pain is only the price you pay for living."

The trappings of the palace had fallen away, leaving just the god and the boy in a void that stretched beyond perception.

"The price too high," said Amit, miserably. "You asking too much."

"Enlightenment is not something only for the spirit, child. The mind must grow too. You don't see that all you do by refusing to live is fo' put you'self back on the wheel of time fo'

suffer again? If you did look more far down you path, you would see that fulfillment come from doing right and then you would tame the wild horse of you passion and guide it to Nirvana, the true pleasure."

Amit looked unconvinced.

The god pressed his palms together. "Follow me now, child. Let we recite the syllable of life and creation."

And from the deep well of Yama's mighty voice, the thrumming musical bass note of the *Om* built up, then rang out, shattering the image in Danesh's mind and leaving him back in the cave with Sedna.

"That was real?" he asked her. "Amit with Yama? That can't be real."

"I think you know the answer. But you not here fo' see truth. You come fo' *hear* it."

Again the world darkened and disappeared.

Before them was Sisyphus the old trickster, pushing his rock up his hill. Sedna stretched her hand out and they flew towards him, like a close up on a movie theatre screen. "Look at he face while he pushing. He ain't got no hope fo' get release. No hope that just one time things gon' turn out different. But even knowing that, he find pleasure in he work, in knowing and feeling he self in action."

"But he was a bad man," Danesh answered. "It say so in the story."

"That's irrelevant. Bad people not allowed to be heroic too? They can choose fo' be the hero in they own story. The real rebellion against this world come from living."

"Listen," said Danesh, "You telling me all these things 'bout death and rebellion and not giving up. Why? What you really want from me?"

Sedna frowned and narrowed her eyes. She raised a hand

and snapped her fingers and Danesh felt himself plunged into ice-cold water. The mark of Zadoq'ua could not protect him from the frigid misery into which Sedna had sunk him. Immediately he started shivering. He opened his eyes and there was only darkness. His Clearsight did not work. He could not swim. He could breathe only in shallow, painful breaths. He sank with no sense of time except the rattling of his frozen bones. Then Sedna's voice came to him. "Look."

Flat, grey rock rose into view. He was at the bottom of the ocean. Veins of orange light rippled across the sea floor. The glow came from just under the skin of the rocky surface – which was shifting and growing. Constantly, the molten insides would burst through a tear in the surface creating booming explosions of black steam before the molten rock from below cooled. Only for another bulge and tear to take place right next to it, making the scene sound like some cosmic factory.

The cold was long gone, banished by the heat rising from below. Something powerful lay restrained under the ocean's barren surface. But was it really barren? No plants swayed down here. There wasn't even any soil. No crabs or fish or – but there was action not far away. In the areas where the water had gone cooler, cylinders of ever-smoking rock ringed the twisting golden orange snakes of the lava.

"There got millions of volcanoes like this," Sedna told him, pointing to the ring of smoke. "Heat from the Earth itself does create and nourish life."

Once he knew what to look for, Danesh could not help but see what was hidden by the surrounding black steam. Life of a kind he had never seen before flitted everywhere – long tubes of red tissue that looked like vertical snakes, tiny worms drifting on the heated waters with mouths full of teeth, bacteria, shrimp, little shelled things crawling along the bottom, blind, eel-like fish on the prowl, even a clam or two. He turned to the floating form of the woman beside him, her clothing streaming in the current. "The whole thing seem so fragile though."

"Them old creature who come to Earth from other places, like Zadoq'ua and Cthulhu and Nyarlathotep, they want we fo' believe that they own this planet. But I say life belong to whoever can sustain it in they self. No matter how humble we start, humans got the same right to this planet. However small we strength against them invader who come from far away, we will fo' live is enough fo' stake we claim."

"But we don't got a chance against them."

Sedna reached behind herself and brought forward the Tablet of Destinies. "No. But we got a way fo' fight. The Dreamtide come from we mind. Human consciousness, all of you together, create it. And it give you power fo' create things like Coral City and fo' master the whole world. The gods and goddesses that people worship get they power from it. And all of that come together inside this tablet. The power fo' change destiny."

Danesh smiled. "So the power inside that tablet mean we got some li'l chance fo' win?"

"No."

"No?" He couldn't believe she had led him through this whole show with Yama and Amit and all that just for a no. "Well what's—"

"They too powerful. If we manage fo' beat one or two of them even, they gon' always be another monster from some outside dimension, some creature with more power than we can ever imagine. But the Dreamtide and the power of creation and the control over destiny, that all give we weapons. We can refuse to accept defeat. We can rebel and be happy knowing we never stop fighting."

"Like the Handsome Monkey King," Danesh said to

himself.

"Yes," said Sedna. "He lose in the end, but he live happy with heself."

"He lose?"

"You don't know the story?"

"I know he didn't think he would win, but I never actually hear any part with he losing."

Sedna's voice shifted to the soft cadences of a storyteller. "Heaven send the Buddha to Sun Wukong, the Monkey King. And the Buddha bet that the Monkey King couldn't escape the palm of he hand. Sun Wukong accept and jump in the Buddha palm and then jump right back out to the end of Heaven. He find five pillars standing there and he pee on them to mark it for he own."

"So he win again?"

"No, because the five pillars was really just the Buddha fingers. When he realise, Sun Wukong try escaping, but the Buddha hold he and turn he fist into a mountain and he seal the mountain with a paper where he write the mantra, 'Om Mani Padme Hum'."

"Oh," said Danesh, disappointed to hear his hero had finally lost. Then he grinned, "But he pee on the Buddha hand at least!"

"Exactly," said Sedna, looking pleased.

From below, the explosions continued, drifting up. They listened as the rumbling merged into a recurring sound. Boom... mmmmbbb. Oooommbb. Ommmmm. Ommmmmm...

The water, the rock, the fire, even Sedna herself dissolved away as the sound seemed to consume everything and then it faded to leave Danesh back where he had started, under the iceberg.

"Danesh!" Medusa called, swimming up from behind

him. "What's the problem? You been drifting here doing nothing for nearly a whole–" She stopped and stared. "Oh, you find it."

He looked down and realized he was holding the Tablet of Destinies to his side, not even feeling its weight.

Another prize to send to the Parliament of Sponges.

Aja called the next day and left a message that Danesh was to sell the cow to a butcher in Affiance. The thought of the animal tied up and having its neck slit made him have trouble breathing. Why was he getting like this? It wasn't just *Aja's* phone call either. At other random times, he would get the dizzying sensation of panic and desperation and a claustrophobic inability to move.

Danesh moved his mother's light-up Om into his room. It was the only way he could get any sleep. The sight of the sacred syllable calmed him. His mother was pleased to see him being so religious and almost forgave him for dropping out of school. "Maybe you could train fo' be a pandit," she had told him once she accepted that he wasn't going back.

Now that he wasn't doing time in his usual classroom cell block, he knew it was only fair that he get a job of some kind, but he couldn't see the point. What Sedna had preached to him about resisting and rebelling in life made some sense, but he couldn't feel it in himself to go find a road in life.

Besides, there weren't any roads under the ocean. Better to let himself float.

He used his free time to read the *Book of Eibon*. That was what the heavy tome from the underground temple was called. Eibon had been a wizard it seemed, one who traded with Zadoq'ua to gain knowledge and power in exchange for being the toad god's servant.

Danesh could tell instinctively what sound each letter was supposed to make and even what the meaning of the words was. But he was still dyslexic, so his readings were haphazard and slow. But his time telling stories and his learning to navigate under Medusa's tutelage had stretched his mind's capabilities, so he found reading to be at least easier than before, if just as painful.

Medusa found him reading the book in his room one night and he explained its origin.

"I don't think he did expect I would take it," Danesh added. "Zadoq'ua give me all these bad feelings fo' frighten me, thinking I would run away from the temple. But I didn't fall for the trick. So now I got a book about he and I can read it."

"But not even the Parliament of Sponges can read it," she said. "They find a copy thousands of years now and they never been able fo' use it."

"I can barely use it meself. Is not the whole book here. Just sections joined up by guess."

"You learn anything?"

"I..." He fingered the corner of the open page. "Don't laugh, okay?"

"Okay."

"I does close me eyes and turn the page 'til I hear them make a sound that seem important. Then I read that p–"

"A sound?"

"Trust me, the turtle teach me how–"

She laughed. "A turtle?"

"You said you wouldn't laugh!"

"Sorry." She sat on the window sill, the breeze blowing loose strands of her silver hair around her face. "So this listening thing work?"

He shook his head clear from admiring her. "Uh, yeah. I think it working because the pieces I read, they connect up and make sense."

"In what way?"

"Eibon work for he for a long time, but he didn't trust Zadoq'ua. He use he powers fo' predict the future and write about what he see gon' happen."

Danesh turned to a page. "Like this here." He read it, saying the words in the speech of Eibon, though they made sense in his head:

> *On a night without dawn the*
> *dark of the sea comes to*
> *end mankind's reign and still*
> *the pulse of Earthly life*

A look of revulsion overtook Medusa's face as he spoke. She said, "I ain't understand it, but the sound them words make is like bones getting grind up."

"The book got a lot of passage sound like that and–"

From outside a dog barked in a sad, begging tone.

"You hear that?" Danesh asked, standing.

"Yes. Why?"

"Is Amit dog. He parents never like Surwa, so they chase he away and he living in the street now."

She looked around his room. "He can't live with you?"

"I feeding he every day, but I can't keep he in the yard. *Aja* allergic."

"You *Aja* not somewhere else right now?"

"Yeah, you right. I can keep Surwa here 'til he come back at least."

"Tell me more 'bout the book. I ain't think you realize how it important."

"Eibon say that a time gon' come when Zadoq'ua gon' get angry because some servant promise he a sacrifice and then try fo' back out from the bargain. Eibon say it gon' make Zadoq'ua decide to wipe out mankind and take over the world."

Medusa nodded to herself. "So that's why Zadoq'ua come back now after all this time." She looked at the book. "Eibon say is who?"

"No, but he put a spell in here. He say it can help stop Zadoq'ua."

"Why? Eibon was he friend."

"Eibon wasn't nobody friend. But he didn't want fo' see mankind get destroy."

"Or he want fo' save he own skin."

"According to Eibon, Zadoq'ua got some of he power in relics in the world up here. He gon' wipe out the people who live near them and come take back that power."

She looked up in alarm. "The temple under the ground that you find the book in. That's the kind of place he talking about."

"Yeah. He gon' kill everybody in Essequibo."

The third quest took Danesh deep under the Pacific Ocean, where he found a wide and bare plain of dirt. He was to find four coloured scales from the Rainbow Fish.

Danesh was surprised that he didn't know this story from the temple. Medusa had to explain as they swam towards the portal. "Lord Vishnu been in the form of Buddha when–"

"The same Buddha from the Monkey King story? He was Vishnu too?"

"Some people think so."

"Wait," said Danesh, "this like that thing you tell me about that time? That different story can be true in the Dreamtide even though they contradict one another?"

"Kinda. The Rainbow Fish did bigger than a whale and it had scales make out of red, blue, yellow, and green. It swallow up Buddha and he only escape because some fishermen kill the fish and rescue he. The meat from the Rainbow Fish feed the whole country for a year."

"So where they put the scales?"

"Most of them, the people make things out of them, magic things. But some still under the ocean."

And those were the scales Danesh now sought. He needed one of each colour. All he knew was the general area they could be found, and he resigned himself to an endless day of swimming around.

Not surprisingly, the man on the turtle showed up. Danesh could make him out clearer than ever and he realized why he looked so familiar. "You's Lord Vishnu, right?"

The figure became instantly more defined. He had four arms, one of which carried a great metal club. His hair was long and black, and he wore a crown and kingly robes.

"My name not important. My job is what matter. I's the preserver of life on Earth. These creatures who invade we from outside, like Zadoq'ua and Cthulhu, they intend fo' end the thing I love most. And I ain't gon' ever let that happen."

"You know where I can find the four different scale?"

"I can't interfere in what you do, but I can stay with you. Just make sure you keep you eyes moving."

That sounded like a hint. His Clearsight was active, and as he swept the horizon, he noticed that Vishnu had a point. Everything looked so much the same in every direction here, that he lost his bearings if he tried to look straight ahead.

They found a few black scales of enormous size everywhere they went. "These from the Rainbow Fish too," explained Vishnu, from the back of his turtle, "But they not useful for magic, so nobody want them. The coloured scales, they been on the top half of the fish. Each colour come from a different element in creation. Blue for ice and water, yellow for lightning and air, green for land, and red for fire. They got the power."

The first coloured scale Danesh found – it was ice blue – lay on the ground in the midst of a swirl of sharks. He had encountered no life apart from very small things for the whole day. Why were there suddenly sharks? Could he dash in and grab it and get away before they saw him? Could he outswim them if they gave chase?

"You could just kill them," Vishnu said.

"What? No. They's just sharks. They ain't do nothing wrong."

"We not concerned 'bout right and wrong. This thing is about survival."

"Well, I ain't got no weapon and I ain't looking fo' kill nobody." Danesh was dressed in his usual seagoing gear of jeans and nothing else.

"You think you can get anything in this world without fighting?"

"I..." he smiled. "Actually, that might be so."

He had noticed that the shark's eyes never moved. Where they looked as they swam their pattern was predictable. And there were blind spots. If he timed it right, he could...

Danesh moved along the silty bottom, keeping his eyes on the graceful white bodies and their curving paths above him. He timed each move to avoid their gaze. Sometimes he had to retreat. Sometimes he had to hold still for longer than felt safe.

But in the end, he was able to pick up the smoothly curved scale, which was as big as a wheelbarrow tray and surprisingly heavy. He removed himself the same way, staying in the blindspots of the sharks until he was beyond their notice and went back to Vishnu's side.

"I still don't see the point of all this," said Danesh, holding the scale before him as he continued his search. "I know I supposed fo' save Essequibo, or the ocean or even the whole world if I do this, but everything I doing, it gon' end up counting for nothing in the end."

"Dying later better than dying now. We got fo' fight hard and fight without no mercy fo' what we can get. We got fo' make them pay a price if nothing else."

"But they not gon' even notice in the end. They so powerful..."

"There ain't got no shame if you weak in this universe. The only shame is fo' give up."

Amit had given up. Was that shameful? No. Just sad.

But why sad? If Danesh really believed all he had said about the uselessness of fighting, why was Amit's death sad?

Because it was the loss of something from the universe. Whatever he was, however long he might have lived, Amit was gone for good and he had denied *himself* the chance to take joy in who he was. And if Amit should have taken that chance, then that meant that the human race deserved a chance to become whatever it could be.

"Good," said Vishnu.

"What?"

"You seem like you got purpose in you now. You moving faster, with spirit. You understand why you need fo' be ruthless now."

Danesh said nothing, afraid that he might set off another lecture about power.

The second scale was green. It was set in the centre of a nest of long twisting vine-like weeds that threatened to snare Danesh's feet. But the movements of the slender vines were dictated by the water's flow and the whole field swayed from one end to the other as the current moved through. Danesh was able to pick a moment when all would be still and swoop down and pull the grassy green scale up and escape.

Now he had two scales, stacked one in the other like plates. He held them before him as he continued swimming. His eyes moved by instinct now, scanning the ground, finding the curved shapes of the occasional black scales and sliding past them in search of the true prize.

The third coloured scale was yellow. It was the property of a colossal squid. The sight made him nearly drop the first two scales in despair. The scale he needed was guarded by tentacles that were thirty feet long and lined with sharp hooks the size of Danesh's fingers. The only good news was that the scale has been set into the squid's tail, at the opposite end from its eyes and tentacles and giant flesh-ripping beak.

Danesh rested the first two scales on the ground and swam up to the squid from underneath. His first challenge was to stay out of sight, yet he needed to approach the calmly moving squid while its large tail fin was pushing water back at him, making it hard to move with any control. At least the tail itself stayed mostly still in the centre, while the flaps on the outside moved. This meant that the scale he needed was not dancing around but moving on a predictable path at the easily accessible top of the tail.

Was the scale embedded in the squid? Danesh didn't want to rip it away and injure the animal. He pushed himself closer.

No. The scale was lodged in a slot, held there by the squid's muscles. The problem was that the squid would notice instantly if Danesh took its treasure from its grasp. At the moment, the tentacles were put away in an upright position, kept still so as to not interfere with the animal's motion. He didn't want to provoke the squid into sending those long tendrils of death after him.

Danesh backed away, returning to the bottom.

"What wrong with you," Vishnu said, his anger visible in his wide eyes and tense shoulders. "You can't give up. Go and–"

"I know what I doing. Relax." He hunted around for a black scale identical in size and shape to the yellow one and then returned to stalking the squid.

He checked the tentacles. They were still dormant. Good. He slid the black scale across the top of the yellow, so that its edge entered the same slot. He nudged it along with care, sending it further into the opening, until it was sitting in position right above the yellow one.

The squid changed direction and Danesh dropped back, keeping himself in the blind spot of its two football-sized eyes. When the squid had settled into a mostly straight line of swimming, he came close again. He used the black scale to lift open the space just a bit and the yellow scale came free almost instantly.

The tentacles curled in alarm, like some grotesque flower opening up, but only for a moment. Soon, the great body of the squid had swum off over the horizon, leaving Danesh with another scale to stack with the first two.

The hunt for the last one seemed pointless, however. Danesh was sure he'd been swimming for days by this point. He was thirsty and tired and impatient and there was nothing to be seen mile after mile except the useless black scales.

When the dark of the sea intruded on his vision, he thought it was just fatigue at first. But then he realized there was a definite point in the grey distance where his Clearsight could not penetrate.

He pointed. "Something over there," he told Vishnu, who had been brooding alongside him the whole time.

"Dagonites," said the god, with disgust. "They got a colony above the ruins of R'lyeh."

"R-what?"

"A city where the Great Old Ones used fo' live. It get destroy by a seaquake long ago, swallowed up and buried. Cthulhu under there still, dreaming about the day he gon' come back and rule the Earth."

"You mean if Zadoq'ua don't do it first."

"You can't see nothing?"

"I can only see dark ocean, like if I been using my normal sight. I think is anything fo' do with them Old Ones, the power fo'

see don't work. Maybe–" He noticed that there were two places of darkness now. There was a smaller cloud of impenetrability closer to him than the great obscure city. He swam for it cautiously, drawn in by what seemed like a light within. Like fire.

From near the surface, he saw the dagonites for the first time. A squad of them were standing like statues, making a circle around the dark water. They were bulky, with smooth scaly heads, thick lips that curved down like a fish's, and no ears. They had grey-green bodies and short arms, and each one was holding a three-pointed spear. Their legs were thick and their feet wide and webbed between the toes.

And in the centre of the dark water was the glowing shape of the red fire scale.

"You should attack them," whispered Vishnu. "You had the right idea before, not fo' attack the squid or the sharks, but them dagonites, they's not Earth creatures. You don't need fo' concern about they life."

"I don't want fight or kill!"

Vishnu held up his club. "I gon' help you."

"You not supposed fo' interfere."

"I don't care. This too important. We can't let them creatures take over we world. We got fo' fight for it."

"No, I can see the red scale and they look like they sleeping. Let me drop down quiet and–"

"No. I fed up with you and you talking – you acting like some frighten li'l boy."

"I ain't frighten, I just–"

But Vishnu was roaring his rage and leaping off his turtle to dive down at the guards below. He swung his club at the first one and exploded its chest in a cloud of dirty red. Immediately, the other dagonites broke out of their slumber and swarmed over to him.

Still holding the first three scales, Danesh abandoned the idea of stealth and swam at full speed for the red scale. He entered the dark patch and the images of the dagonites turned to moving shadows. He slid the scale into the stack with the others and bounced off the muddy seafloor, pushing for the surface above. He knew where the portal would be. All he had to do was outrun the dagonites. They looked like good swimmers, but if he had enough of a head start, Medusa would be at the portal to help him fight–.

As soon as he emerged into the light above the dark water, he found himself bracketed by three dagonites. The one in the centre thrust his spear at Danesh underhand and he pulled back and to the side, avoiding the three points of the trident. The second dagonite threw his trident and Danesh avoided it easily, swimming hard to the side. But then the last dagonite brought his spear down in a fierce two-handed blow.

All Danesh could do was protect his belly with the scales. His arms shook to the bone with the impact of the weapon. His injured ribs felt the force of the blow as if they'd been hit directly. And then the scales shattered. He saw it as if in slow motion: cracks spread through the smooth surface from three impacts, joining and then widening, then the three spear points broke through and the four scales shattered into bright coloured shards that slipped out of his hands and drifted in the water.

Even as Danesh despaired over his failed quest, the fight continued. He twisted away from the tridents and fled. The three attackers kept after him. Danesh looked around for a hiding place. Nothing. No cave, no weeds, no boulders. He dodged a spear thrust and turned. There. The colossal squid from earlier was swimming at an angle far above them.

Danesh made for it, approaching the tail from below with the three dagonites right behind him. He timed the attack so that he slammed into the squid's tail and upended it. The gigantic body spun around and its hook-filled tentacles spread open just as the three dagonites stopped to avoid crashing into it. They were helpless as the thick, thirty-foot long tendrils whipped out and curled around them. They stabbed at it, but the hooks were so deep into them that the squid probably could not let go even if it wanted to.

One by one, the squid drew them deeper into its face, where its great beak chomped into them. Danesh watched a leg severed at the knee float free from the misty blood of the fight.

But not even a great creature like the squid was invulnerable. The sharp points of the spears had punctured it in many places. Goo and blood and strips of flesh were streaming from its body in a dozen places. The three dagonites and the squid stayed locked together as they sank slowly, landed on the sea floor, and died.

When the last twitch had left the squid's body, Danesh went over and searched the corpse. It had died from many grievous wounds that now stank of poison. Danesh was sure that this was how the whale on his beach had died too, killed by the dagonites.

But unlike the whale, the squid's death was his fault. He wanted to cry as he watched the ruins of the magnificent creature. He turned away and the black scale caught his eye, still embedded in the squid's tail. He reached for it, easily pulling it free from the lifeless flesh.

Vishnu approached. Bits of skin and flesh were trailing from his club. Behind him, the darkness had dissipated, leaving more wrecked bodies. Danesh could see the details of their numerous bludgeon injuries with absolute clarity now. And the great turtle was dead too, lying on its back with two fins ripped off.

"You kill three of them?" asked Vishnu. "Like you stronger

than I expect."

"This ain't nothing about strength!" Danesh pointed at the scattered bits of coloured scale littering the battleground. "This trial was for me. Fo' show everybody that I could help beat Zadoq'ua. Now all this killing end up being for nothing because I fail. Why you bother helping me with Sedna and Polyphemus and then do this?"

Vishnu seemed to realise where he was for the first time, like a man waking up from a dream. He saw the dead squid and horror crossed his face. "I ... Oh, no ... This isn't..."

"Forget it." Danesh swam away and began placing the shards of coloured scale into the bowl of the black scale. He didn't know if crumbs would be enough to satisfy the quest, but he hated the idea of leaving the sparkling remnants behind. Some of the pieces were as big as his palm. Others were smaller than a fingernail. He searched them out and piled them in the black scale.

Vishnu came over, a stunned, ashamed look on his face and began picking up pieces, putting them in the 'tray' without comment. Danesh resented his presence since he had caused all the problems in the first place, but he doubted he would have been able to collect all the fragments without Vishnu's help.

At least he felt it was all. Eventually, they could find no more and Danesh accepted that he had to return to Coral City and admit his failure.

"Useless," Bejara exclaimed when Danesh and Medusa came before the council.

No one else at the table spoke. Even Numah just stared at the ground where Danesh had placed the broken scales.

"You can't blame he for what somebody else do," said Medusa. "If it–"

"That don't matter," said Bejara. "The point is he ain't somebody can help we fight Zadoq'ua. And he lucky I don't ask the council fo' kill he now just to make sure."

"They wouldn't listen to you cruel ways."

"Quiet, girl. You weak just like you mother."

"My mother did strong more than anybody in the Abyss!"

"She was a traitor!" said Bejara, leaning forward on her fists, like a gorilla.

Watching them face off, Danesh realized that Bejara and Medusa were the only two silver-haired fairmaids he had ever seen. But the mystery of their link failed to intrigue him now that everything in Coral City tasted of failure. He turned and walked away.

"Stop!" said Numah. "The council ain't release you, Danesh. You fail the test and we got fo' keep you here 'til–"

He looked back defiantly. "I's not you enemy. You should know that after everything I do. You real enemy coming for you soon. Worry about he."

Numah signalled to Daphne and the other guards and they started readying their *dakis*, but the Apexa tapped her stick lightly and they backed off. Danesh walked to the nearest wall and pushed his way through then swam away from the seascraper and took the portal home without once looking back.

For a week he did nothing but stay in his room. Surwa kept him company when his mother was out and couldn't complain about the dog. He ignored phone calls from the butcher who had bought the cow from *Aja* and was expecting delivery. For the last two days he even ignored calls from *Aja* himself, unable to explain to the man who had taught him to be practical in life that he felt too much pity for a cow to let it be killed.

Except it wasn't pity. He continued to be terrified by the sense of being trapped and violated every time he imagined the cow being tied up for slaughter.

Robot and Kevitt stopped by after school one day with Nadira, greeting him with forced smiles as they invaded his room.

"What y'all come here for?" he asked.

Robot gave him a playful push on the shoulder. "We

come see if you still going to the Ravi B concert with we this weekend. You been talking about it for four month now. You and Amit couldn't shut up ab–"

Danesh took a sharp intake of breath at the mention of Amit. The others looked at Robot like he was an idiot. Nadira especially seemed ready to tear off his head.

"This not the right way fo' deal with this," Kevitt said to Danesh. "You can't lock up you self in here. You got fo' accept that Amit gone and get back to life."

"He right," Nadira said. "Amit was me friend too. I not gon' let that–"

Robot scoffed, "You only going because you want make smile face pon Sir Karan–"

"Stop quarrelling!" Kevitt shouted. "I trying fo' explain something."

But Danesh didn't need any explaining. Accepting Amit was gone was actually the easiest thing for him. He knew now that the universe was a vast swirl of events with no reason or purpose. There was no need to rationalise his friend's death in any way. Life and death didn't have to make sense. But the loss still hurt.

"Just go," he told them. "Enjoy you'self. I alright here."

They put their heads down and started leaving. At the door, Kevitt looked back. "You not coming back to school either? Miss Geeta already telling everybody that she know you never had the brains fo' make it through school. You can't give up. Education more important than silver and gold you know."

That last bit was a favourite line of Kevitt's, something his parents had repeated to him since before he could talk.

Danesh thought about how much he had learned out there in the wild Dreamtide, how much bigger life seemed than the walls of his school. He shook his head regretfully. His prison time was over.

Medusa finally visited on Saturday, just after midnight. His parents had gone to the concert in Anna Regina, so he was alone. "You get Numah and Bejara so vex," Medusa told him, chuckling. "I never see the two of them agree pon nothing, but they went together fo' tell the Apexa fo' put you in a cell and keep you there."

"That why you come, fo' kidnap me again?"

"No. I just want see how you doing." She held up her bare hands. "See, I ain't even bring my *daki*." She looked around. "Where the dog? I thought he living with you now."

"My mother chase he away this afternoon. He in the village somewhere. What happening with the war?"

She left the window and sat near him on the bed, their knees touching. "A couple other cities get attack, but nothing heavy. Is like the dagonites just testing fo' see how we would react. But no big movement like we did expecting. Is like Zadoq'ua waiting."

"For what?"

"Nobody don't know." She pointed at the floor where Eibon's journal rested. "What that say?"

"Just that Eibon make a spell fo' fight Zadoq'ua power and it can only work one time and that Zadoq'ua gon' rise up when he find the person who betray he."

Medusa looked thoughtful and then asked, "It say whether the betrayer human? Or if it could be a woman?"

Danesh leaned in and rested his head on her shoulder. He was vaguely aware of the feel of her smooth skin against his face and the way her scent tickled his nose, but that didn't matter now. She was the only person he trusted in the world – who he felt comfortable enough with to let show him comfort. He asked, "You think the traitor might be Bejara? Because the Abyssians used fo' had dealings with the dagonites and now she want fight them all of a sudden?"

She shifted her shoulder so his head could rest more comfortably. "Maybe, but she don't fit because Zadoq'ua know where fo' find she, and he ain't rising—"

"You tell the council I got this book?"

"Yeah. Bejara say that there ain't no way a boy smart enough fo' read a book like that."

"So they don't believe you?"

"Well, actually..."

He pulled his head upright and looked at her. "What?"

"The Apexa is the one who send me here tonight."

"Fo' take the book?"

"No. She say if you find the book and you can read it then it must be you who *supposed* fo' read it and she want me fo' make sure you doing you work."

He laughed and took Medusa's hand in his. "Tell the old lady I done with schoolwork."

"She also say you not safe here, so if you want, you can come back with me and bring the book. I got the carriage down at the beach so it won't get wet."

Danesh smiled. "You really want me fo' just leave this place and go live with you?"

She bit her lip as they looked at each other. Their faces drew closer.

Downstairs, a great pounding started on the door.

"Who downstairs?" Medusa asked, pushing him away with a hand on his chest.

"Nobody. Just—"

Then there was the sound of a door slamming open and a man shouting. Was that *Aja's* voice? Footsteps pounded up the stairs.

"Quick," whispered Danesh, opening up the wardrobe door, "hide!"

Aja tried the handle of Danesh's door and found it locked. "Danesh!" he shouted. Then the door burst open, its flimsy little bolt flying across the bed. Danesh's grandfather followed right after, his boot coming down from his kick. "What going on with you, boy!? You ignoring you own *aja* and think–"

He caught sight of Medusa still trying to fit herself into the wardrobe.

"O-ho!" *Aja* said, eyes bright with savage joy. "A fairmaid. You father tell me something suspicious been going on all this time, but I never imagine–"

"You know about fairmaid?" Danesh asked.

"I been hoping fo' get me hand pon one of them for a *long* time." The old man moved with a speed Danesh had never seen before, lunging at Medusa. She kicked him in the chest. It barely slowed him, his eagerness overpowering her.

"Stop," shouted Danesh grabbing at his grandfather. *Aja* pushed him back, amazingly strong, and Danesh crashed against his dresser.

Aja reached for Medusa's legs and grabbed at her thigh pouch. She twisted away, but he came up with a length of rope and before she could reach the window, he tackled her and bound her feet, tapping on the metal to pull the rope ends tight.

"How you know fo' do that?" Danesh asked, fighting to stand as his burning ribs restricted his breathing.

The old man tapped the top of Eibon's book and said with a grin, "I learn a lot of things in this world. You think just anybody could beat up a femaid? I know how fo' deal with animal like she." He reached for more rope.

"No!" Danesh grabbed his wrist.

"Leave me alone, boy!"

"She's my friend."

"Really?" *Aja* pulled Medusa wrists together as she struggled and he bound them with another piece of rope. "Then tell she fo' stop fighting."

Danesh reached over to tap in the unlock code, but his grandfather slapped him. Stunned, he looked up and saw *Aja's* eyes glowing with mad power, like twin fires. Was his grandfather even human anymore?

"You want get in my way?" The old man asked. "Alright then..." He dragged Medusa though the door and carried her down the stairs while Danesh chased after them. At the back door, the old man unhooked the sickle and put it to Medusa's neck. "You want me kill she right now?"

"No, don't do nothing."

"Then stay quiet."

Medusa stopped fighting too, respecting the potency of the serrated blade.

"Listen to me, Danesh," *Aja* said. "This girl, she can fix everything that gone wrong for me these years. I need you fo' help me. Help you family."

"She don't know nothing."

"Is only she blood I need. Zadoq'ua been after me all these years because I do the first sacrifice wrong, but I can make up for it with she."

"You can't—"

"Stay quiet and come with me, or I kill she right here in front of you."

Aja made Danesh walk in front and they headed for the sandy bank near the koker where the fishing boats would all be parked. Danesh's boat was the only one that would have an engine attached, since the little 15HP Mariner wasn't worth the effort to steal. *Aja* dropped Medusa in the small boat and pulled his arm back, holding the knife.

"Don't kill she!" said Danesh.

Aja smiled reassuringly, the same smile that had once been charming. "I just putting it away fo' help you push." Together they eased the boat into the channel from the dry shore.

As soon as *Aja's* boot hit the water, the face of the Chinese Rolex on his wrist shattered, spraying glass. Medusa flinched and took a deep breath. *Aja* looked at his wrist and shook his head in resignation. "I guess Zadoq'ua know I in the water now." He sat behind Medusa at the bow, the sickle by her neck. "Come, boy, start that engine. We got fo' get this sacrifice over quick."

"*Aja*, what's all this you talking about sacrifice and killing people? You sounding crazy and you acting—"

"I say start the boat! Stop acting ungrateful!"

"What you mean ungrateful? What you do for me that I must help you kill a girl?"

"Carry we up the coast and then cross over to the watchman house by the island."

Danesh complied, his eyes switching between the engine, the knife at Medusa's neck and the water ahead.

"You uncle was the first one who figure out how fo' read that book," said *Aja*, sounding like he was telling a boyhood reminiscence rather than an explanation of murder. The fire in his eyes had gone out as he calmed down. "He tell me he could hear a voice explaining it. But he ain't understand everything."

Aja cleared his throat and spat over the side. "Anyway, he get all excited, say that there had this power fo' be rich and run the world that Zadoq'ua could give we if we kill a child for he. The only problem is Janak didn't realise how the thing really work, so when we do it, we do it wrong."

"You been in that killing too, *Aja*? I thought was Uncle Janak."

"Yes, you uncle kill the boy – catch he, tie he up and pull the knife cross he neck. This same knife here in fact. But when the blood spray out, is I been there, holding you up so you could get the blessings."

"Me!" Danesh's whole body trembled in terror. He gripped the handle of the outboard motor for support.

"Who you think I do it for?" The old man laughed. "You was just born. And I think how I could make you life so easy. But it turn out that the sacrifice wasn't fo' bless you. Was fo' mark you fo' serve Zadoq'ua. And when I realise, I say no way. I ain' giving me grandson fo' be no slave to no monster."

"My father had any part in this too?"

"Nah. He too stupid fo' understand them things. Ever since he was growing up. Is you uncle I teach about Zadoq'ua and the Old Ones and all that. He's the one I bring in the circle with me fo' worship Zadoq'ua when he was just a boy."

They were halfway to the point where they would turn away from the coast to cross over to the island. Danesh saw Medusa curling her legs under her, looking for something to press against. He said, "So all this is why you stay away from water all this time? Stop being a fisherman?"

"Yeah. We send the sacrifice through the sea. Zadoq'ua know fo' look for we there. Had fo' stop being near dog too. Any time I come close, they try fo' bite me."

Medusa spoke, her voice grim and accusing. "Animals and Zadoq'ua got kinship. Them dog know you's he enemy."

"I wasn't looking fo' be no enemy. I just want a good life for Danesh."

"For me?" Danesh stood, wiping tears of rage from his eyes. "You kill a li'l child for *me*?"

"Don't complain about blessing in this life."

"I don't want it!"

"Well, good. When Zadoq'ua come, you can tell he. In the meantime, I gon' sacrifice this one here and pay back the debt I got."

"But she's just a femaid. They got millions of them. You think Zadoq'ua gon' value she blood?"

"He value it with that li'l boy and there got millions of children in this world too. Is youth and magic he want. He want fo' see people potential get cut short. I try fo' buy me way back before when I kill you *aji*. But it didn't work. The ocean didn't accept she."

"You kill *Aji* Meena too?!"

The old man ignored him and twisted Medusa's head, exposing her neck. "But this one here, she young and she fresh and I can feel she just full with power. I can–"

Medusa braced her feet against a cross board and leapt up, head-butting him before he could react. He staggered back and the knife fell onto the deck. With her hands and legs bound Medusa could do little against him except keep knocking him off balance.

Danesh banked hard right and revved the engine, heading straight for the shore which was just fifty feet away.

Both Medusa and *Aja* fell with the maneuver and were slow to get up – Medusa because of her restraints, *Aja* because he was hunting for the knife.

The boat struck the shore with a thudding lurch and drove deep into the wet sand, the bottom erupting upward in broken planks and splinters. The impact tossed Medusa into the air just as she was gaining her feet and she spilled over the side. Danesh jumped out to join her and knelt at her side. He loosened the rope and she kicked it off.

Aja stood, holding the sickle again, and jumped onto the sand, landing drunkenly on one knee. He was breathing hard through a pained grin. It was like he was taking joy in the madness of the moment.

"Don't let she escape or–"

A growl from the dark trees erupted into a bark and Surwa charged out and bit his hand. The knife fell and he pulled away, but the dog would not let go. *Aja* kicked Surwa three times before he got free and then scrambled around to the other side of the beached and broken boat.

Danesh had released the ropes holding Medusa's hands behind her back and she grabbed for the sickle.

"No," he said in horror, "Leave that!"

"This is a weapon of Zadoq'ua. We can't leave it." She picked it up, the blade's serrations catching the starlight like a row of teeth.

The three of them – boy, fairmaid and dog – ran back up the beach. Medusa led them to where her egg-shaped cargo carriage was waiting. She threw the sickle into it and pulled her *daki* from the side where it was strapped. "Time fo' show the old man what a real fight is," she said.

"No. No more fighting. Let we just go."

"He attack me."

After a moment of desperate thought, Danesh said, "The Apexa gon' want fo' know about this. You can't waste time fighting."

Medusa looked at him, resentful of his common sense. She looked back at *Aja*, who was half running, half limping in their direction. She grabbed the carriage. "Fine. Let we go."

"Hold on." Danesh tapped the side of the carriage and called to the dog, who was still on the beach.

It whined.

"Surwa, come!"

Aja was closer now, shouting incoherently. The dog

looked at him then plunged into the water and got into the carriage. Medusa's tail splashed the water and she disappeared, hauling the dog. Danesh took one last look at his *Aja*, who was standing on the shore with a look of rage and desperation, then he turned and swam away.

They emerged from the portal to find that Coral City wasn't there. The landscape was the same, but where the towers should be reaching towards the surface, there was nothing but open water and wisps of darkness, like the clouds left behind after a thunderstorm.

"This not right," said Medusa, stunned. "This not supposed to happen. We prepare we self. We did ready."

"The dagonites been here," Danesh said. "They bring the Dark with them. They destroy the city."

"Bring the carriage." Medusa swam ahead, too fast for Danesh to keep up. She held her *daki* at the ready as she circled lower to where Coral City had once stood. Danesh followed, dread in his stomach.

He could see dead fairmaids floating in the water, many gashed and missing limbs. Some seemed to have been bitten open.

There were dead dagonites too. But there were no living enemies for Medusa to fight. She let out a cry of frustration and embedded the point of her *daki* in the back of one attacker's corpse. Inky, black liquid poured from the wound.

By the time Danesh caught up to her, however, she was back in control and her focused eyes were scanning the battleground. Medusa pointed. "See the dome tops?"

This close, he could see that the *mojh* buildings had sunk so that only their tops were resting on the bases.

"They use all the *mojh* from the walls fo' strengthen the tops so we can defend the people better."

It had only helped them a little though. All the buildings showed damage. Some had been ripped into and were now flooded.

And there were even more bodies floating in the spaces between the domes. Sharks circled underneath like vultures.

"Don't move!" Bejara and a handful of her Abyssian troopers floated behind them.

"What happen here?" asked Medusa, swimming up to her. "The city was ready for war! We should've never defeat like this."

"We prepare for dagonites," Bejara said, keeping her *daki* pointed at them. "But Zadoq'ua come too. And he had the whole ocean of them, on the way to war. They ain't stay and finish we off. Just pass through and keep going, like we wasn't nothing."

"Zadoq'ua he self?" asked Medusa.

"He going for *Aja*," Danesh said to her. "He know where fo' find the traitor now. That's what he did waiting for all this time."

"What this one talking 'bout?" Bejara asked, still haughtily refusing to make eye contact with Danesh.

"We find out Zadoq'ua plan," Medusa said.

"He gon' destroy Essequibo," Danesh said, "and then he gon' come find the relics that got he power in them,"

Bejara's façade of arrogance slipped to reveal a face of worry. She looked around warily as if expecting another attack. "Come with me." She led them to a gap in the coral reef that would be invisible to anyone looking from just a few yards away. It led into a long tunnel that ended in a wall of *mojh*. Inside the wall was a bare cave. Numah and a few Coral City soldiers were inside, talking. Other tunnels led away from the cave in different directions.

"What you bring them here for?" Numah asked Bejara. His robe was spattered with blood and sticky green entrails. Over in one corner, the Apexa lay unconscious on a mat while priestesses tended to her. Daphne stood guard over the scene, looking exhausted.

As Medusa related their encounter with *Aja* and the information from the *Book of Eibon*, Danesh finally had a chance to let Surwa out. The dog stayed close to his side, and Danesh sat on the ground and stroked its neck.

For the first time since being attacked by his grandfather, he had a chance to dwell on what he'd learned. A boy had been murdered for his sake. He watched the reflection of the cave's light on the sickle as Medusa showed it to Numah and Bejara. He shivered at the thought of what that blade had done. His stomach churned. He pictured himself as a baby, gurgling happily as innocent blood sprayed over his face.

Danesh could hold back no longer. He leaned onto his hands and vomited over and over, until there was nothing left but the sour taste of his spit.

He regained his senses to the feeling of Medusa rubbing his back and speaking softly. His vision cleared and he found he was sitting on a boulder while Numah and Bejara looked down on him.

"Don't baby him," Bejara told Medusa. "Danesh, we got time fo' stop all this. Zadoq'ua not part of the Dreamtide. He can't use portals. He got fo' swim thousands of miles before he get to you home. Leave now and you can stop he."

"Me? You's the soldier."

"You got the spell book and you know how fo' read it. And you got this." She held out the sickle to him.

He scrambled backwards. "I ain't touching that thing!"

"This thing got Zadoq'ua power inside it, just like you. If you use it, you can hurt he. This might be the only weapon in the whole world what can do that."

"That thing kill a li'l boy."

"How much children you think Zadoq'ua gon' kill if you don't stop he?" Danesh thought of Clarendon. He even thought of Robot and Nadira who were technically still children. Danesh himself was a child. It wasn't fair for him to be responsible for–.

No. Fairness wasn't something he believed in now.

Medusa turned his head to hers, holding his face in her two soft hands. "I know it hard, but you would feel worse if you ain't try. I gon' come with you."

"All of we coming with you," said Bejara, standing with her troops behind her. "All who left fo' fight anyway."

Daphne nodded as if to herself and stepped forward.

"We need you fo' guard the Apexa," Numah told her.

"The Apexa give me the duty fo' guard the surface boy. Only she can tell me otherwise."

"I speak for she when she–"

But the look of determination she gave him stopped his objections.

Danesh breathed in and stood, his knees still weak. He reached out and took the handle of the sickle, then used the cord to hang it from the belt in his jeans.

Three hundred soldiers followed Danesh out of the portal and into the waters near Tiger Island.

They were attacked immediately by swarming dagonites. *Dakis* and daggers flashed alongside the tails of the fairmaids as they responded by getting into formation, meeting the assault with gritted teeth and determination. Daphne alone held back, keeping her position near Danesh.

"Get the book," Bejara ordered Medusa as the chaos of battle roiled the murky water. "We gon' hold them back."

Danesh was paralysed by the violence before him. Each time he saw the glint of a blade in action or blood pouring from a wound, he could only picture his grandfather holding the sickle. Medusa shoved him in the back and the three of them started for shore.

A pack of five dagonites broke off to chase them.

It was a close race. Twice, Medusa and Daphne had to drag Danesh along to keep him from being grabbed by the reaching claws of a fish monster.

"We far enough from the main fight," Medusa said to Daphne. The bodyguard nodded her understanding and braced to take on their attackers. The dagonites incoherent screams of bloodlust broke into his head as they attacked. Medusa dodged to the side and attacked their flanks. Daphne stood between them and Danesh, keeping them at bay with jabs of her *daki*. One jab skewered a dagonite through the neck where it wriggled until Daphne pulled the spear back. The injured creature grabbed its throat with a terrified expression as it drifted up.

Medusa had slashed open two of them already, their blood clouding the water. Instant kills. Even as the sight revulsed him, Danesh felt his hands drawn to the weapon tied to his waist.

No. He couldn't touch that. It was a tool of murder.

But the power would feel so good another part of him knew. He would be an agent of death instead of living in fear of it.

His temptation ended when the fairmaid warriors finished their fight, Daphne stabbing her victim through the chest. Medusa slashing open the spine of the other dagonite.

There were no other pursuers as they swam to the shallows.

They broke the surface to find a night sky. "This not right," Danesh said as they climbed the boulders of the sea dam and looked around. It should have been a bright Sunday mid-morning. Instead, people were gathered around candles in the open bottom flats of their houses, talking with neighbours.

"Stay here," Danesh told Medusa, "People gon' start scream if they see you." He walked casually up the street towards his house.

"Danesh!" shouted Clarendon, running out from his yard. "Where you been? Everything going crazy."

"I know. Stay with you parents 'til it over."

"But they not *doing* anything. They just stand up talking 'bout how the phone and the radio don't work. I want come with you and the blue lady."

"Blue what?" He turned to find Daphne at his side. "I tell you fo' stay back."

"You tell *Medusa*, not me." Daphne looked around, on alert.

Danesh turned to Clarendon still reaching for an lie to tell the boy but he was already running back home, shouting, "Mommy, Danesh bring home a magic lady!"

Danesh stepped through the open front door of his house behind Daphne, looking around for signs of *Aja*. She led them up dark stairs with just the moonlight from outside to guide their steps. Danesh looked backward, expecting the old man to ambush them, before he entered his room.

The *Book of Eibon* was where he had left it on the floor. He was just opening it to search for the spell when a line of darkness caught his eye through the window. A thin streak of nothing was blocking the horizon – the dark of the sea in full power.

Zadoq'ua's attack had begun.

Danesh raced downstairs and back out to the old seawall, his bodyguard right behind. The ocean was drawing away from the shore at a speed Danesh had never seen before. It left exposed mud visible for miles out. Standing in the swamp were a few dozen dagonites. They were swaying in the wind as if hypnotised. Further out, Danesh didn't need his Clearsight to see what approached. A giant wave was building up, rising to twenty feet and still climbing as it sped to shore.

"Find the spell," said Medusa.

"I ain't know is which one."

"Just guess like you do before."

"I ain't guess. I listen to–"

Right. He stood straight up with the book before him and closed his eyes. He turned the pages back and forth, hoping to hear the familiar sound that came with finding the right passage.

"Hurry."

He breathed in, relaxing, and then ... a gentle, low whisper hit his ear. He looked down to see a page with its writing glowing red. The book had never done that before. He knew this was the spell meant to stop the attack that was unfolding against him and everything he had ever known.

The top of the massive wave gleamed foamy silver on the far horizon as the wall of dark water built and coiled towards the shore. It still had some ways to come – there was a mile of muddy, exposed shore where the ocean had been sucked out to feed the approaching tsunami.

The spine of the heavy *Book of Eibon* dug into his hip as he tried to rehearse the words before he said them. It didn't work. Every time he started from the beginning the words seemed to be different. Was that his dyslexia or just how the spell worked?

Didn't matter. He had to say it out loud in one reading.

He had to focus with precision on what he was doing, without actually thinking about what he was doing. Execute each word on instinct without thinking about the way the letters felt on his lips. It seemed impossible, like zigzagging a path across the protruding rocks of a swamp where the rocks were actually alligators and if you lingered too long, they would sink away or simply bite your ankle off for your insolence.

He said the first syllable. Then the second. The words began to sputter out of his mouth. As he approached a quarter-way down the page, thunder rolled overhead. Without looking up, he could tell the clouds had thickened above. Flashes of lightning began to light up the clouds.

So many distractions. He forced himself to keep reading. It did no good. The thunder was constant now. It was ... it was calming. The sound that penetrated was a rumble that reminded him of the 'ommmmmm' of the sacred syllable, the way Yama has spoken it in his vision. The musical thunder built as Danesh approached the last sentence, sparks spearing down around him.

He shouted the last line of the incantation and the glowing letters caught fire despite the rain. He dropped the book and it ignited, burning quickly into ashes that were whisked away in the storm winds.

Parallel streaks of golden lightning fired down from overhead, like a curtain along the line of the coast. Just as they were about to hit the sea dam, the bolts curved forward and shot out across the mud and struck the tsunami.

The entire wave lit up in gold for a brief moment and then steam exploded up from it, obscuring what Danesh could see. A few seconds later, with the air smelling of electricity, he saw the wave emerge from the clouded horizon. At first, he was disappointed to think he had failed, but then he realised the wave was not as high and was actually dying down.

It still had some speed, however, and Danesh saw that while he had prevented annihilation there was still danger. The water came in like an enormous tide, taking back the exposed mud and climbing against the sea dam. It became so high it started pouring over the top and even then rose higher. The flood swept down the other side of the dam into the village, filling the drains and then the streets and the yards.

And with the flood came a new danger. Dagonites started leaping over the wall and wading into the village. They chased after the people roaring mindlessly. Danesh half-swam, half-ran towards Clarendon's house and yanked the trident away from one fish-man just before he attacked the screaming boy.

The dagonite turned, screeching, and backhanded Danesh into the water. He lost the trident and the dagonite came at him. Daphne leapt in front of him and brought her *daki* down in a

182

two-handed strike that plunged the dagonite into the water, dead. Two more dagonites came at them. From either side. Daphne turned to take the closest one.

Insitinctively, Danesh gripped the handle of the sickle. He had only to cut the cord that held it to his belt and he could wield its power. Already he could picture the blade slicing into the flesh of the creature before him, sending it into oblivion.

Clarendon was still crying in fear, cowering halfway up the stairs that rose to the second floor outside his house. The sight of the crying boy made Danesh freeze with guilt, the murderer's weapon in his hand.

The second dagonite flung his trident full force and struck Daphne through the back and out of her chest just as she had finished off her first opponent. She made a low groan as she staggered and turned, looking down with disbelieving eyes at the blood spurting from the wounds and then she fell, lifeless, into the shallow water, the shaft of the trident sticking up.

Danesh dropped the sickle back to his side, stunned at the cost of his hesitation.

The dagonite was moving, however. Straight at Clarendon. Danesh pulled the trident from Daphne's corpse. He raced between the monster and Clarendon and stabbed it in the thigh. It splashed backward, off-balance, taking the weapon with it.

Danesh grabbed Clarendon's hand and pulled him up the outside stairs of his house. At the landing, he lifted the boy and pushed him onto the zinc-sheet roof before following. He held Clarendon while he looked around at the battle from the top of the house.

The surge of water over the wall was petering off, but the village was inundated in waist-deep water. Dagonites were everywhere. Bejara and her people had arrived and were hunting them down. Villagers' cries of terror and despair were coming from every direction.

"This ain't the end," said a voice.

He turned. Vishnu stood there, looking tired.

"You right," said Danesh. "I got fo' go help." Clarendon was looking at the stranger in awe. Danesh told the boy, "You need fo' stay up here where it safe. I gon' go–"

"No," said Vishnu. "Zadoq'ua not here. You got fo' go find he out there."

"But the people here need me."

"You can help them more by leaving. Don't make the same mistake I make at R'lyeh. You had the right idea then. I didn't think ahead, I just fight the enemy I see in front of me. *You* got fo' think ahead now. You can't let Zadoq'ua get any of he old power back."

Danesh looked at Clarendon then down at the village. He looked north to where the concert was supposed to be, miles away. Dagonites were probably attacking there too. And his mother and father were there. Robot and Nadira and Kevitt too. He wouldn't be able to save them in person.

"Go," said Vishnu. "I gon' help here in the meantime. Only you can stop Zadoq'ua."

He found Medusa fighting a dagonite near the spot where the smoke shack had been before the wave had washed it away. He drew the sickle from his belt to help her as the creature shoved its trident at her head. She dodged, bending at the waist, then stabbed it under the ribcage. As it choked up oily, black blood through its fish lips, she shoved it off her blade with her foot and it tumbled backward down the rocks to the ocean.

She turned with a savage expression to check for more enemies, her braided hair swinging wide. Danesh remembered with shock how frightened he had been of her in the beginning. All this time he had spent with her as his guide – talking, exploring and laying his head on her shoulder – had lulled him into forgetting that a ranger of Atlantis was a warrior above all else. Now he saw the killing instinct in her again and instead of being scared, a thrill of desire was throbbing up his arm from the blade in his hand. He wanted to join her in the joy of destroying their enemies and–

She grabbed his shoulder and shook him out of his bloodlust. "Danesh!"

He dropped the sickle back into his belt, feeling like it had poisoned him. His head cleared and he looked up.

"We got fo' get to this tomb where you find the book. We can't let Zadoq'ua get there first," Medusa said.

"He not going there."

"How you know that?"

"Remember when *Aja* kidnap you? He say take the boat to the island."

She looked out to the sea. "The church!"

"Yes. That's why we find that dead goat there. Is a sacrifice place for Zadoq'ua."

They approached the silent churchyard through the abandoned rice mill, using the bulk of the rusted equipment and its brick walls to hide them as they crouched.

Two dozen hooded figures formed a ring under the silk-cotton trees in the front yard of the church. They were chanting. Danesh caught fragments of their words on the wind:

...Cthua t'lh...lgh thok!

G'llb-ya, Zadoq'ua!

Y'kn'nh'...

He said, "That must be the rest of *Aja* people who does worship Zadoq'ua."

"They know he coming?"

"Actually, I think they calling he."

The men stepped back and knelt, raising their voices. Near the centre of the circle Danesh saw one man, his hands and feet bound as he knelt in the dirt.

"*Aja.*"

"Stay here," said Medusa. "You can't fight all of them."

"I can't stay here and do nothing." He stood and she pulled him back down.

"The thing Zadoq'ua need, the relic, it got fo' be in the church. Let we go round the back and find it while they busy."

They found a trail behind some bushes and set out, struggling to control the squelching noises of their feet in the muddy ground.

A hollowness took shape in the air at the centre of the cultists' circle as their chanting grew louder. It was like a hole in reality itself, taking the outline of a great hulking creature. Danesh felt he could see through this shimmering opening to the far side of the universe itself. Rushing stars appeared amid darkness and his mind froze at the vision of infinite distance and time.

Just when he was sure he would go insane from the contemplation of his own insignificance in the cosmos, the three-story-tall figure of Zadoq'ua coalesced into reality. The screaming cries of the cultists became ecstatic, as if they were weeping in joy.

Zadoq'ua pointed at *Aja* and spoke, his words lost under the chanting. And *Aja* answered back. Though he couldn't make out the words, Danesh could tell from his swaying motion and beseeching tone that even now he was bargaining, looking for an angle to come out the winner.

Danesh couldn't leave him. No matter what he had done, he loved the old man. Medusa gave him a pleading look, but Danesh shook his head. He turned and walked across the bridge, right towards Zadoq'ua. She gave a frustrated grunt, then set her *daki* at the ready and followed him.

The cultists saw them immediately but made no move to attack. Instead, they spread out in two ranks, like a V, welcoming him.

"That's she!" shouted *Aja*, looking from Medusa to Zadoq'ua and back. "I can give she to you, Master. I gon' promise to keep serving you and–"

"But she here now," said Zadoq'ua mockingly. "How you gon' promise me what I got already."

Medusa said, "You ain't got nothing, you big toad. You might kill me, but you ain't never gon' own me."

"I could make you eat you own lips if I say so. In fact, how about–"

A deep rumble sounded on the other side of the church, out towards the ruined estate house and the mangroves by the ocean. The familiar deep hum blasted in, sounding like a mixture between a low horn and chanting congregation.

Ommmmmmmmmmmmmmmmmmmmm!

A giant figure strode out of the darkness, silhouetted against the stars. From its shadowed face, a beam of intense white light shot out and struck Zadoq'ua in the chest, throwing him backwards.

The attacker came closer and again fired another blast, preceded by the same *Ommmmmmmmmmmmmmmmmmm!* as before. The beam was wide and pure, except near the edges where it frayed into prismatic colours.

Now the giant was close enough for Danesh to see that it was Polyphemus. He stepped into the clearing, dressed in armour, with the Tablet of Destiny strapped across his breastplate. Danesh could tell it was him despite the fact that he wore a full black helmet – the same smooth black as the fish scale that Danesh had recovered in R'lyeh. The helmet was curved like a welder's mask in front and the top resembled the smooth head of a dolphin. Where an eyehole should have been, the pipes of the syrinx had been set instead, facing forward like gun barrels of random lengths. And the helmet sparkled with the red, green, yellow, and blue bits of scale that had been embedded in it.

The cyclops looked down. "Hey, Danesh, my friend."

"Polyphemus? What you doing here?"

"The Parliament of Sponges send me. I come fo' show Zadoq'ua he not the only one with power in the world."

"You can see now?"

"The helmet let me find things with sound."

Polyphemus took a giant stride towards where Zadoq'ua

was rising to his feet and blasted the old god again. And knocked him down again.

A cry behind Danesh made him spin around. *Aja* had gotten free and was attacking Medusa. She held him at bay with her *daki* and he turned to the cultists.

"Help me catch she. The master not gon' be happy if you let she get away."

Though he had been a traitor just a few minutes before, the men seemed confused at seeing their monstrous lord being attacked and they fell back on habit, obeying the old man. Each of them drew a curved dagger from within their robes and closed on Medusa.

Danesh ran towards her, but she shouted, "Go help Polyphemus."

"He don't need help," said Danesh, looking over at the giant pair, "he winning–"

Zadoq'ua used his large, long legs to leap up over the next attack by Polyphemus and flew at the giant's head. He landed on his shoulders and drove them both into the side of the old mill, knocking over a vine-covered brick wall.

Zadoq'ua pointed backward to the church bell and the top of the tower erupted in a fountain of thick, black liquid that poured down the sides of the stone, coating it. The inky, black slime spread out at the base of the structure and individual figures started to rise out of it, separating themselves from the muck. They looked vaguely humanoid, but with sharp edges and flat bodies that stretched at inhuman angles. They raced along the ground together, twisting like a flock of birds.

Ommmmmmmmmmmmmmmm! sounded again from Polyphemus' helmet and Zadoq'ua brought his wide jaws down over the giant's head. Before his jagged rows of teeth could bite, a blast of light struck him in the back of the throat and sent him flying backwards. He tumbled and slid right into the bell tower. The impact created a crunching sound and then the tower imploded. Amid the dust and collapsing bricks, the large, black bell clanked its way down and rolled out onto the grass.

The ink creatures swirled together and rushed at Polyphemus. He swept his beam of white light through their ranks, cutting many of them in half. But the separated pieces stretched towards each other like flowing liquid and knitted themselves back together. The swarm of black figures slashed out at Polyphemus with arms like ribbons of liquid steel, cutting at his legs and knees.

He roared and backed away kicking at them in vain.

Danesh drew the sickle and ran towards the fight. The hunger for glory and the infliction of pain that the knife provided charged his body with energy making him run faster. He fought the emotion down, trying to prevent it from taking over his mind while still using it to his advantage. Hanging on the edge between control and rage, he brought the knife up. The curved blade was hot and glowing so yellow that it seemed golden.

Danesh swung it sideways at an ink creature on the outside of the pack. The blade unfurled, like a liquid whip of light and slashed through a dozen of the amorphous imps.

Stunned and exhilarated, Danesh looked at the sickle. The blade was back to being solid, but it vibrated with the urge to lash out again. Before him, the ink creatures writhed in pieces, this time unable to reform themselves.

He grinned and slashed at the crowd again with the flickering light-whip the sickle had become. More of the ink shapes died as it sundered their forms. The rest flowed away and then around him. He fired at them, beating them away, but they kept trying to find a way through.

Over by the front of the church, Danesh caught sight

of Medusa, battling *Aja* and his cultists between and around the trees. She was never able to concentrate on one man enough to make a decisive strike, but her speed and claws and whirling blade made them regret every attack they made. Already, three of them were too wounded to stand properly. But she was not invulnerable. Her *mojh* showed scars in several places where it had healed over from cuts to her body. Luckily, the protective substance acted like a bandage too, keeping her from bleeding.

Zadoq'ua rejoined the fight with a roar from his wide, slobbery mouth. He lunged at Polyphemus and knocked him back before slashing him with his three-clawed hands and leaving deep, red gashes.

Polyphemus grabbed the great toad by one stubby arm and swung him to the ground. With Zadoq'ua recovered, the ink creatures shifted their attention away from Danesh and back to the Cyclops. Danesh, sensing this change, kept beating them back from Polyphemus, denying them space with his whirling blade-whip. There seemed no end to them, however, no matter how many Danesh destroyed. He noticed that new ones seemed to slither out from under the bell constantly, like the drip of a leaking tap.

And while they might be able to keep fighting forever, he could not. Not even with the rage of the sickle driving him. He wondered how long he could keep feeding off the energy of the blade and not lose himself to its mindless desire to kill. In the back of his mind, he kept seeing the image of the crime this blade had committed and it terrified him to think he could follow it into such acts.

Beyond Danesh and the ink creatures, the two giants sought to destroy each other, knocking over sections of the old estate house, caving in the roof of the church and even cracking trees open. Zadoq'ua was clearly more powerful and seemed to be winning, but the frequent blasts of creation light from Polyphemus' helmet would stun him thoroughly each time it hit. Even the ink creatures froze whenever Zadoq'ua suffered a strike of its searing power.

It reminded Danesh of the way all the programs on a computer would lock up when the CPU was overloaded. He dodged an attack by a leaping ink creature and slashed its gleaming body in three as it sailed past. He turned to see the next attacker hesitate as Zadoq'ua took another blast of pure light. It almost seemed like the ink creature's brain disconnected. Like it had no instructions to follow in that small instant so it did nothing.

The image of a computer network came to Danesh. Zadoq'ua was controlling all the creatures, but he was routing the signal somehow. Danesh used his whip to slash a path through the shadowy spawn of Zadoq'ua so he could get to the bell. This was the relic Zadoq'ua came seeking. Danesh was sure now that it was a tool to control armies of servant spawn.

Zadoq'ua leapt past Polyphemus and crouched down in Danesh's way. He held a hand out to Danesh and started closing his fingers together, like he was squeezing the air. Intense pressure bit into Danesh's head and he felt his mind being taken over.

"Polyphemus!" he struggled to shout. "I got fo' get to the bell. Get him out the way!"

Even as the cyclops lowered his head to fire his helmet beam, Zadoq'ua dodged, deceptively quick and kicked him in the knee, then grabbed his wrist and tossed him at a tree. He landed against a bare, jutting branch which impaled him through the side of his stomach.

The time Zadoq'ua took to get rid of Polyphemus was all Danesh needed, however. His mind was free from Zadoq'ua's encroachment and he rushed forward. When he was close enough, he swung his fire-whip at the bell, wrapping the burning blade around it. Zadoq'ua used his powerful legs again and leapt at Danesh, claws out, jaws wide.

With supercharged strength, Danesh swung the heavy bell up and out. The fire from the whip had engulfed the whole thing and the flaming mass exploded against the side of Zadoq'ua's head and knocked him onto the ground. Great Zadoq'ua lay with his round belly in the air as pieces of the shattered bell burned around him. Everywhere, the twisted shapes of the ink creatures stood still, each like the sculpture of a man driven insane.

The cultists were retreating, helping each other limp away. Some of them had their hoods off and he could see they were men he knew, who he had thought of as ordinary people. His old teacher, Sir Karan was among them, looking frightened and lost. Only *Aja* remained in the clearing, pleading for his life on his knees as Medusa pointed her spear at his throat.

Polyphemus kicked his way free of the impaling branch and fell to his knees. The great helmet of light fell forward onto the ground and rolled away. He unstrapped the armour with the Tablet of Destinies and held back the blood of the exit wound with his hands.

Zadoq'ua groaned and turned over, then rose with undignified awkwardness into a crouch. One eye had gone inflamed and red and a starburst scorch mark stained his temple. His mouth drooling, Zadoq'ua said, "You can't win."

Danesh knew he could keep fighting all night. He was like Sisyphus with his rock, in it to the end. But there were other people in the world besides himself.

"I think you know that's a lie," said Danesh. He held up the glowing whip. "I know I hurt you more than anybody ever hurt you before. You *know* this weapon got the power fo' finish you off if I keep fighting."

"Then why you holding back?"

"Because I don't know if I can kill you for sure. And I don't want fo' spend the rest of the night seeing if I gon' win the fight."

Zadoq'ua stared at him. "You want a truce?"

Danesh waved at the island around them. "You really want fo' rule this place? You could be back safe in you cave again, learning about the universe."

The great toad stared down at him, nostrils slowly flaring.

"People dying right now," Danesh continued. "People who ain't need fo' die. How 'bout if I don't kill you and you go home with all you pets and don't never come back?"

This time Zadoq'ua answered him. "I can't leave empty-handed. Give me the old priest as sacrifice."

Danesh looked over at his grandfather, still under guard by Medusa. "No."

"He's a murderer. I know you creatures ain't got much of a life, but murder is still a serious crime to you. Give me the old man and I gon' give you power and knowledge."

"Like what you gave *Aja*? No."

"He break a promise to me."

Danesh said, "Well, I gon' make you a new promise. Something that actually useful."

"What promise I could ever want from you?"

"I gon' give you this sickle and let you take it away from this Earth so nobody gon' ever be able fo' use it against you."

Across the clearing, Polyphemus looked up in surprise. To his right, Medusa seemed ready to object.

Zadoq'ua said, "And you trust me not fo' just kill you when I get it?"

"I ain't know you enough fo' trust you. But Eibon say in he book that you always keep you word."

"If you keep the knife it gon' protect this world from me

forever."

Danesh smiled sweetly. "But you not gon' be coming back, remember?"

"I see," Zadoq'ua said, nodding his understanding. His wide lips twisted into what might have been a smile. "A hard bargain. But I gon' say yes."

Zadoq'ua stretch out his palm. An invisible force gripped the sickle and pulled gently. A part of Danesh's mind – the raging, lustful part that had cherished each cut and lash he made during the fight – did not want to let go. But he looked over at *Aja*, the man who had shaped his life from the start in ways that were terrible and disgraceful, and Danesh knew he could never trust himself with such a weapon. He uncurled his fingers and the sickle flew into Zadoq'ua's grasp.

Even as he caught it, the great toad was fading out, showing again that window to an infinite beyond before disappearing. Overhead, the dark sky went grey, then white, then blue, revealing the midday sun above.

Polyphemus joined Danesh and Medusa as they bound *Aja* with her ropes. "I know you do what you do for you people, fo' keep the fighting from hurting who you love, but I ain't agree with it."

Danesh didn't answer. He was too busy trying to avoid looking at *Aja's* eyes.

Medusa said, "We get Zadoq'ua fo' leave. We safe from he fo' the rest of we life. I think is a good deal."

"Mhmm," said Polyphemus, surveying the wreckage of the battleground. "But them old ones, them don't never stay gone."

EPILOGUE

"Look, another one!" Danesh pointed as the meteor streaked low over the north-east sky.

"Is how much is that?" asked Medusa. They were lying on the inclined roof of a house that had been abandoned after the flood six weeks before.

Danesh shrugged. "Seven? Eight?"

"I thought it woulda had more by now. You say this Perseid thing is a shower."

"You ain't impressed?"

"Sorry, no."

"Is alright. I know you live in a place where everything exciting."

"Is not that, really." She sat up. It was dark all around. Many people had moved out of this stretch of coast. The rice crops had been ruined by the salt water and the roads and foundations of the houses had been undermined. They were alone. Medusa looked at the cloudless sky. "The thing is, everything seem so far away, is like I don't feel connected to what happening up there, you know?"

"Yeah," said Danesh, glumly. "I starting fo' feel that way 'bout the water."

He had not visited Coral City in a month. His Clearsight and his ability to swim and breathe underwater had faded away to nothing. He doubted he would ever visit any of the wonders of the ocean again. And that made it all feel less real. Even *Aja*. His grandfather was sitting in a prison cell in the caves under Coral City, serving a life sentence and already he could feel his memory of the man fading.

"How Surwa doing?" Danesh asked.

"He think he's the boss of the place now. He and Alpata. I still can't believe how good the two of them get along."

A dog and an octopus, best of friends. That was an image

that would stay vivid in his mind, he hoped. "And Bejara gone back to the Abyss?"

"Yeah," said Medusa with relief.

"You know, I get the feeling you and she got a big story behind—"

"That was between she and me mother a long time ago. Over a hundred years. It don't matter now."

"How long?"

"Hundreds of years. Before I born."

He looked her over, trying to convince himself she didn't still look his own age. "That's how long y'all does live?"

"Yeah. Except a lot of rangers does die more young."

He nodded. That was one of the reasons Medusa would not be visiting him again for a long time. Her responsibilities were vast now that she had been promoted out of training. "I think you gon' live longer than the rest," he said. "You don't try and make everything into a fight."

"You think people gon' come back here?" Medusa asked, pointing at the rows of empty homes.

"Oh, yeah. Fast too. This place been getting flood out since forever and people still here. They like Sisyphus, always pushing they rock up the hill no matter how much they get knock down."

"So you gon' go back to school?"

"No."

"But you can't give up." The look she gave him confirmed in his mind that she was not planning to see him again. She was trying to set him straight before she left. "I thought education important up here?"

"That school give up pon me long before I left. Besides, they got other ways fo' get education."

They watched the stars fall until the night began turning to dawn. Danesh declined to accompany her to the water. It was too painful to get so close to the edge and know he had to remain on shore. From his rooftop, he watched her walk out against the lightening sky to the sea dam. A nearby rooster was calling the world to life. Medusa waved at Danesh. He waved back and then she swam into the water and dove beneath the waves.

He watched the spot where she had disappeared, wondering if that would be the place where she showed up again, however long it took her to return.

He would probably be an old man by then. And she'd probably still look like a teenager. Life really wasn't fair.

He laughed as he watched the rooftops around him start to glow in the yellow sunrise.

Of course life wasn't fair. That was the one lesson he'd learned in all this. Life was just struggling. The only guarantee was that there was something weird and wonderful down the line and you just rode the bumps as best you could and hoped you didn't fall off before you got to the good stuff.

AUTHOR'S NOTE

St Peter's Church is a real place. However, it's actually located on the island of Leguan, not Tiger Island. It is quite pleasant to visit ... in daylight.

Coral City is also a real place. It's just hard to get there.

ABOUT THE AUTHOR

Imam Baksh is a writer from
Guyana. He enjoys tales of
magic, monsters and heroes
of all kinds. He's interested
in history and how the world
works and enjoys research.
His debut novel, *Children
of the Spider*, won the 2015
Burt Award for Caribbean
Young Adult Literature and
his second novel, *The Dark of
the Sea*, won the same prize in
2018. He is also a three-time
winner of the Henry Josiah
prize for his short fiction for
children.

TALES FOR YOUNG ADULTS
FROM BLOUSE & SKIRT BOOKS

ALL OVER AGAIN
BY A-DZIKO SIMBA GEGELE

GROWING UP IS HARD. You know this. And when your mother has X-ray eyes and dances like a wobbling bag of water? When your father's idea of fun is to put all your money in a savings account and make you get up at 5 am every Sunday morning? When Kenny, Percival Thorton High's big show-off, is after Christina Parker – your Christina Parker? And when you have a shrimp of a little sister who is the bawlingest little six year old girl in the whole of Riverland? Then growing up is something you not sure you can manage at all. Who in their right mind could? Who? You?

All Over Again is an enchanting slice of boyhood. It is a charming coming of age story with a bold narrative style that pulls you into it.

Winner of the 2014 Burt Award for Caribbean Literature and longlisted for the 2015 International IMPAC Dublin Literary Award.

CHILDREN OF THE SPIDER
BY IMAM BAKSH

MAYALI IS A GIRL on the run. Driven by desperation and the search for her father, Mayali leaves behind everything she has ever known on her home world of Zolpash, a land of sulphur and harsh weather, and journeys to Guyana. There she meets Joseph, a boy without the gift of speech but with much to say. Together they go on a daring, cross-country adventure to save earth from the invading Spider gods and their armies. Will their warning come too late? Will anyone even believe them? And will Mayali be able to find her father?

Children of the Spider is a fast-paced adventure. The story moves from the lush hinterlands of Guyana through to the bustling city of Georgetown where the colonial past continues to rub shoulders with the gritty, contemporary world. It is a refreshing take on Caribbean myth and mythology from an interesting new voice.

Children of the Spider won first place in the 2015 Burt Award for Caribbean Literature.

DANCING IN THE RAIN
BY LYNN JOSEPH

TWELVE YEAR-OLD ELIZABETH is no normal girl. With an imagination that makes room for mermaids and magic in everyday life, she lives every moment to the fullest. Yet her joyful world crumbles around her when two planes bring down the Twin Towers and tear her family apart. Thousands of miles away, yet still touched by this tragedy, Elizabeth is swimming in a sea of loss. She finally finds hope when she meets her kindred spirit in 8 year-old Brandt and his 13 year-old brother, Jared.

Brandt and Jared, two boys as different as Oreo and milk and just as inseparable, arrive on the island to escape the mushroom of sorrow that bloomed above their lives in the wake of the tragedy. Elizabeth shows them a new way to look at the world and they help her to laugh again. But can Elizabeth and Brandt help their families see that when life brings showers of sadness, it's okay to dance in the rain?

Set against the dazzling beauty of the Dominican Republic, Dancing in the Rain explores the impact of the tragic fall of the Twin Towers on two Caribbean families. It is a lyrical, well-crafted tale about finding joy in the face of loss.

Dancing in the Rain won a Burt Award for Caribbean Literature (2015) prize.

TALES FOR YOUNG ADULTS
FROM BLOUSE & SKIRT BOOKS

GIRLCOTT
BY FLORENZ WEBBE MAXWELL

A WEEK AGO, Desma Johnson had only two things on her mind – in exactly eight days, she would be sixteen years old and to top it off she was inline for a top scholarship, bringing her one step closer to her dreams. Life was perfect and nothing would get in the way of her birthday plans. But it's 1959 and the secret Progressive League has just announced a boycott of all cinemas in Bermuda in order to end racial segregation.

As anxieties around the boycott build Desma becomes increasingly aware of the racial tensions casting a dire shadow over the island. Neighbours she once thought were friendly and supportive show another side. So, Desma must learn that change is never easy, and even when others expect small things from black girls, she has the right to dream big.

In this startling debut, Florenz Webbe Maxwell takes a little known fact about Caribbean history and weaves an engaging tale that speaks eloquently to the contemporary experience. *Girlcott* takes you beyond the image of Bermuda as a piece of paradise and charts a narrative of resistance, hope and the importance of fighting for change.

Girlcott won a Burt Award for Caribbean Literature (2016) prize.

DREAMS BEYOND THE SHORE
BY TAMIKA GIBSON

17-YEAR-OLD CHELSEA Marchand was pretty satisfied with her life. Until recently. Willing to play the dutiful daughter as her father's bid to become Prime Minister of their island home brings her family into intense public scrutiny, Chelsea is swept along by the strong tidal wave of politics and becomes increasingly disturbed by her father's duplicity. She finds a reprieve when she meets Kyron, a kindred spirit encased in low riding blue jeans. The two share a bond as he too struggles to get beyond his father's shadow.

But when Chelsea discovers an even darker more sinister side to her father's world, a discovery that makes her question the man he is and the woman she wants to be, she must decide how much of her own dreams she is willing to compromise to make her father's come true. But can she find the strength to stand up to her father and chart her own journey?

Tamika Gibson serves up a fascinating and stirring debut novel about growing up and accepting who you are, regardless of who your parents may be. Buoyed by the rhythms, heat and lyrical lilt of contemporary Trinidad and Tobago, Dreams Beyond the Shore is a heartwarming story declaring that decisions matter far more than destiny.

Dreams Beyond the Shore won first prize in the 2016 Burt Award for Caribbean Literature.

TALES FOR YOUNG ADULTS
FROM BLOUSE & SKIRT BOOKS

A DARK IRIS
BY ELIZABETH J. JONES

IT IS 1972 and 12-Year-old Rebekah Eve is excited to be on her way to the prestigious Meridian Institute with her best friend, Wanda. But Rebekah's joy is dampened by her parents' separation. She misses having her father at home and the fun things they did together. Most of all, she dislikes her mother's new 'friend' – Thomas Forster – who is trying way too hard to win her over. Life gets even more complicated when her new friend Zende is arrested for the attempted assassination of the Governor.

To cope, Rebekah turns to her art. But her paintings take on new, or rather 'old' life, as figures from the past seep in and replace her usual subjects. She is thrust into a whirlwind of emotion as her visions and the resulting paintings unveil wounds of the past that are not buried as deeply as some would like. With help from the mysterious Lady of the Library and her new art tutor Mr. Stowe, Rebekah makes sense of these visions and unearths the truth behind one of Bermuda's legends. But some truths are difficult for anyone, especially a young girl, to digest. Ultimately, she must learn to trust herself, believe in her talents, and that even a little black girl from a small island, could one day become a famous artist.

A Dark Iris seamlessly combines the historical novel with magical realism as it explores history and identity. It was a finalist for the 2018 CODE Burt Award for Caribbean Young Adult Literature.

MY FISHY STEPMOM
BY SHAKIRAH BOURNE

JOSEPHINE LOOOVES CRICKET! The game, her dad and her best friend Ahkai are the only things that make living in the very, very, veeery boring village of Fairy Vale, Barbados manageable. She really wants to play for the school team, but Coach Broomes says only boys are allowed. Josephine knows she can play better than any of the boys in the team, if she could just get a chance. To make matters worse, her father has a new girlfriend, Mariss.

No matter what anyone else says, Josephine knows there is something 'fishy' about Mariss. She is just too perfect. And maybe it's all the stories about baccoos and douens, and other mythical creatures from Miss Mo, champion fish de-boner of Fairy Vale, or maybe it's all the missing pets, but Josephine begins to suspect there is something downright spooky about Mariss. But will she be able to get to the bottom of the mystery?

My Fishy Stepmom is a hilarious offering of from Barbadian author Shakirah Bourne. The novel serves up a wonderful offering of Caribbean fantasy fiction. It was a finalist in the 2018 Burt Award for Caribbean Young Adult Literature.

TALES FOR YOUNG ADULTS
FROM BLOUSE & SKIRT BOOKS

THE BEAST OF KUKUYO
BY KEVIN JARED HOSEIN

FOR THE SECOND time in her life, 15-year-old Rune Mathura comes face-to-face with a brutal murder when her classmate Dumpling Heera goes missing and is eventually found dead. Dumpling's murder drags the small, rural village of Kukuyo into the national spotlight, showing a darkness curdling in the town. But Rune knows that the memories of the villagers and police are short. Inspired by her love of detective television shows, she launches her own investigation.

Yet, Rune soon learns that real life is not the same as television and neither justice nor evil appear in black and white. Her journey takes her along a bloody trail of chicken feathers, down a muddy ravine and into a grimy den where Rune encounters dark secrets and a terror that is very, very real.

This gripping mystery comes from the pen of one of the Caribbean's most potent new voices. Kevin Jared Hosein is a winner of a Commonwealth Writing prize and has been twice shortlisted for the Small Axe Literary Prize for prose. *Beast of Kukuyo* was one of the winners of the 2017 Burt Award for Caribbean Literature.